Raves for the work of
SEYMOUR SHUBIN!

"First-rate writing, marvelous characterization, believable dialogue, intelligence, gripping suspense that never lets up until the thrilling denouement…A rare find that contributes to the notion that we are experiencing a new Golden Age of mystery writing."
—*Jonathan Kellerman*

"Shubin understands that the recipe for good fiction is set in stone: (1) grab reader by throat; (2) squeeze till limp."
—*Philadelphia Inquirer*

"[Shubin] has brought off a bizarre and blistering rarity… Expertly handled."
—*Newsweek*

"A masterfully written dark crime novel…It deserves to be up there on the same shelf as James M. Cain's *Double Indemnity*."
—*Dave Zeltserman, Hardluck Stories*

"Shubin's novel is recommended as a must for those who like their fiction with the explosive qualities of a 16-inch shell."
—*San Francisco Call*

"The tension never lets up."
— *Dorothy Salisbury Davis, MWA Grandmaster*

"Shubin's terse prose lends a noirlike quality to this engaging suspense tale...A first-rate story, sharp dialogue, and a compelling lead character make this a standout."
— *Booklist*

"A masterful job."
— *ForeWord Magazine*

"Seymour Shubin has an enviable knack as a novelist, the ability to combine a philosophical plot with some of the finest action writing you'll run across in American literature."
— *Oklahoma City Oklahoman*

"[A] superb mystery."
— *The Snooper*

"Shubin draws his characters with precision inside a tense, suspenseful plot that moves to an explosive finale. It's a powerful story."
— *Los Angeles Daily Breeze*

"Riveting suspense and intense human feeling... compelling and convincing."
— *Greenwich Time & Times Mirror*

The snow was beginning to come down even harder now but he could see that the sky ahead was almost a summer blue. He began looking on the weather more and more as the proper crazy setting for what he was doing. And the questions he'd been trying to suppress ever since he started this drive were coming back like hammer blows.

What if I find out I did kill her? What then?

He almost closed his eyes to the splattering snow and the sweeping wipers.

But it can't be!

Then why are you going back there?

To clear his head of it once and for all, he kept telling himself. To be free in a way he hadn't been since that day.

But then why did a part of him want to turn the car around?

He was aware all at once of how slowly he'd begun to drive, as if to make this last hundred and fifty miles stretch on forever. And, even though reluctantly, he stepped a little harder on the gas...

WITNESS
to MYSELF

by **Seymour Shubin**

A HARD CASE CRIME NOVEL

A HARD CASE CRIME BOOK
(HCC-019)
April 2006

Published by

Dorchester Publishing Co., Inc.
200 Madison Avenue
New York, NY 10016

in collaboration with Winterfall LLC

ISBN 0-8439-5590-2

The name "Hard Case Crime" and the Hard Case Crime logo
are trademarks of Winterfall LLC. Hard Case Crime books are
selected and edited by Charles Ardai.

Printed in the United States of America

Visit us on the web at www.HardCaseCrime.com

For Talia Grace Levine

WITNESS TO MYSELF

Chapter One

I had no idea how tormented he was. None. And what torments *me* is wondering if I could have helped him. I mean, from the time he was a kid, when we were both kids.

Alan and I were cousins, the only children of two sisters. We lived for quite a few years in the same neighborhood, in fact only four houses apart. And being five years older, I was like a big brother to him, more than just a cousin. He used to enjoy being in my company, following me around, which I took on as my role even though once in a while, like all little kids, he was a nuisance.

Of course things changed as we grew older, as we followed separate careers, different interests. But we still called and saw each other now and then; and when I got married, he was my best man.

So what torments me is that maybe—no, not maybe, surely—I could have helped him, starting when he was a kid, been a true big brother. And then, later on, surely there was a clue here and there to his troubles, all of which I missed not only despite our closeness but despite the books and many articles I have written on crime.

I tell myself now that I should have done this, that, or whatever. But one of the things I'm not sure about is whether I would have advised him to make that trip to Cape Cod or just let things be.

I do know from what he told me that for almost every mile of that trip he was torn apart by doubts.

Turn back, he kept telling himself. Turn back, turn back.

You don't have to know if you killed her, he told himself. You've lived all these years, fifteen years, without knowing. And you've got a good life that you're going to destroy, you're only thirty, a lawyer, you have someone you love, and a new career, one where you can do so much good. You've never had it better. For God's sake turn around!

He told me that when it really hit him like this he was only about ten miles from home, had some three hundred more to go. But despite his pleas to himself he drove on, trying to assure himself that he could turn back at any point. And what's more, even if he did go on it wasn't as if he was going there to confess. And the point was, there might be nothing *to* confess. He really didn't know if he'd killed her; hurt her, yes, he'd hurt her, but killed her? He was sure he hadn't. He'd run from the scene in terror, falling, jumping up, running on, a kid in horror at himself, a fifteen-year-old kid who had never knowingly hurt anyone in his life, afraid at that moment that he'd killed her, but then gradually, back in his home and over the years that followed, sure he hadn't.

Except at those times when he wasn't sure, and a flame would sweep through his whole body.

It was winter, mid-February, but the highway under the bright sky was free of snow except on the shoulders and on the dark limbs of trees. And it was pretty much free of cars.

He wasn't even sure how he would find out. The answer lay in one of the towns on Cape Cod, South Minton. He had found out the name of the newspaper there, the *Cape Cod Breeze*, a daily, and had looked it up on his computer, trying to go back to July 8, 1989; but the paper's Web site only had stories as far back as '92. And he hadn't seen anything about such a crime in the handful of other newspapers throughout the state he'd been able to find online. Nor had he seen it, on the several occasions he'd dared to look, on any of the "unsolved true crime" shows on television.

So how did he expect to find out now? The newspaper office was one way, of course, and if not there, the public library, or maybe a paper in another town up there. But all of these options could be risky, might arouse suspicion, even though he would ask for papers starting way before that day and ending way after.

He just had to know.

He felt as if he couldn't go on any longer with Anna, or even with his new work, if he didn't know.

His eyes kept checking the gas: It was getting low and he would have to stop soon. Only at that moment did something strike him, although of course he had known it all along—that this was the same highway they had taken, his mother and father and him, in that motor home they'd rented.

And he remembered the three of them even, yes, singing.

Chapter Two

Actually, it was completely out of character—both Alan and I agreed on this—for his father to rent a mobile home. His parents had moved out of Philadelphia and into the suburbs when Alan was eleven. They had also owned a summer house in the Pocono mountains, about seventy miles away, so they used to spend most of their vacations there, sometimes with us. But then they sold it and his father came up with the idea of renting one of these mobile things for about a month, starting off by visiting a few East Coast beaches and then heading into Maine and up to Cape Cod. It was a large motor home, some thirty feet or so. My aunt was hesitant at first: He was sixty and had never driven one before except for a short practice run at the dealer's. But as it turned out there was to be no problem with that; even she drove it a little. No, not with that.

My uncle had been forty-five—and my aunt thirty-nine—when Alan was born, which I mention because their ages came to worry Alan as a small boy, mainly because they were much older than his friends' parents. He had learned about death firsthand when our grandfather died, and at first it scared him that one day, without fail, he would be in a coffin. But then his concern began to focus on them, that they would die long before him.

My uncle was a lawyer, mostly in real estate law, and my aunt a stay-at-home mom. From what Alan used to tell me, he was sure he was going to be a lawyer too, though not in his father's specialty—somehow it came to him that he would be a criminal lawyer. And the way he talked about it to me, it wouldn't be about saving criminals but saving the innocent. But oh how that was to change.

They were rich though not, except in my mind, super-rich. After leaving our neighborhood for the suburbs, they lived in an area of fairly large homes, ones with long circular driveways. Alan began going to private schools. The best friend he had as a small boy was a kid named Will Jansen; in fact, as he told me, he didn't think he ever loved any friend more, though he was never to see him again after moving out of our neighborhood, except once, much later, on a television interview program. He remembered them doing so much together and talking about everything, except —strangely, though perhaps not—about what was happening to their changing bodies as they entered adolescence, about the strange new directions Alan found his boyish fantasies taking.

His father—Alan didn't even *think* of talking to him about sex, undoubtedly because his dad had never talked to him about the subject. Alan looked on him simply as a hardworking, brilliant man who lived for his mother and him. And his mother, in his mind, was asexual. In fact the only thing he remembered her ever saying to him that had any kind of sexual connotation was a remark she made one time when she looked up from the newspaper she was reading and, out of nowhere (though it probably had something to do with what she had been reading), said to him, "It's important that you treat a girl like a flower. Like a flower." And that was all; she went back to her reading, and it left Alan so uneasy, as though she'd said it to something dark inside him. Nor did I, his big-brother cousin, ever say anything to him; it was easier not to, and in a way, as I see it now, it was as if I was protecting him, the way I used to protect him, say, from crossing the street on a red light. And so when, late in grade school, a certain tall, ungainly half-idiot in special-ed, Henry, would come up to him and other kids in the schoolyard and grin with large teeth and make fast, long strokes of his clenched hand in the air, Alan had no idea what it meant. Until one day, alone in the gray silence of his house, he found out. It was the end of his childhood, and the start of a new phase of his life characterized by bewilderment and self-loathing.

As I was to learn, Alan often envied me because my mother was smart-looking, "modern," dated frequently between marriages and laughed loudly. And he couldn't help envying me because I was allowed to do things he never could, like go to overnight camp or live with friends in Italy one summer when I was only twelve; and though I lived apart from my father it seemed in

Alan's eyes that I went to just about every kind of ball-game with him. But it was just to a few.

Now I don't want to give anyone the idea that Alan was some kind of creep as a kid. He was good in school, was never so much as scolded by a teacher, never lied that I knew about (his mother had an expression, "A liar and a thief are the same thing, they steal something from you"), was a decent athlete: fairly tall, skinny, he was on the soccer and tennis teams in high school. Unlike me, he didn't smoke pot or, except for a few experiments, cigarettes; had friends, though none he felt he could really open up to about what was troubling him about sex; they all seemed so confident. By the time he was fifteen he hadn't gone out on a one-to-one date but had been to some parties and church—Lutheran—dances, though he could never relax when he danced, was stiff and uncomfortable. He'd never kissed a girl, except when he was a kid at one of those spin-the-bottle things.

His father worked late most nights, coming home after Alan and his mother had dinner, and he took a lot of business trips. But he occasionally took Alan to a ballgame, and he generally saw to it that they went fishing on at least the first day of trout season. He gave Alan a good feeling about reading, and neither he nor my aunt made a big fuss about him watching too much TV. My uncle was tall, six-feet, slender, with gray-streaked brown hair; Alan sort of looked like him, though he had black hair and was a little shorter, about five-eleven.

My aunt was of medium height and a little heavyset, with a round pretty face and short sandy hair that was gradually turning gray; a good cook and housekeeper though she always had a twice-a-week maid. She used to tell Alan stories about her childhood, always happy ones, but once in a sudden burst of tears she told him she'd had a miscarriage a few years before he was born: late enough so they knew it was a girl. It was the first and last time she ever mentioned it. But Alan often thought of that little girl who would have been his older sister.

That flower.

Chapter Three

Alan stopped at the first service station he came to and filled the tank and bought a bottle of water at its so-called mini-mart. As he was pulling out it began to snow, tiny dots at first on the windshield and then heavy splatters. He found himself wishing it was the start of a blizzard, that soon he wouldn't be able to drive on; but that, he told himself, was crazy, he could turn around at any time. But in any event the snow stopped shortly; he had driven under a black bloated cloud and now was in sunshine again.

The weather had been perfect every day of that trip fifteen years ago but the trip itself had started off wrong. For one thing, he was angry at his parents and at himself. They had come to him with the idea of this vacation as if it were a done deal, when he had a first-time job he was looking forward to as an assistant sports counselor at a day camp.

"Come *on*," his father said, "you've got your whole life to work. Don't ruin this, we're a *family*, it's probably something we'll never do again."

"But you could have asked me, couldn't you?" he demanded. "You could have at least asked me!"

"Alan," his mother said, "don't raise your voice. You always raise your voice."

"I'm not raising my voice." Always, it seemed, he was being warned about a fiery temper he didn't know he had. And this would only make him angrier. "I'm just talking, I'm just making a point."

"Well, then just talk," she said.

Eventually he gave in without much more of an argument than that, though the feeling of being treated like a baby, hardly anything new, smoldered in him.

And then, the second way it started off wrong was that his mother and father had a fight only about ten miles into the trip.

They hardly ever fought but when they did it was as though, to him as with most kids probably, his world was in collapse.

This time it was over something as trivial as his father's sunglasses.

His father asked her as he was driving to get them out of the glove compartment. When she couldn't find them he said, "You put them in there, didn't you? I asked you to."

"Well, I did."

"Then they're in there. Look for them again."

She went through the compartment again. "No, they're not. You must have taken them out. Try to remember."

"Don't tell me to remember. I didn't take them out."

"Bob, please. Check your pockets."

"I told you I didn't take them out." But he patted at his shirt and then dug into his pants pockets. "I don't have them. Now you try to remember. Did you really put them in there?"

"Of course I did."

"Well, they're not there and I don't have them!"

"Then they must have fallen out of your pocket."

"Christ, will you stop that? I told you I never took them out!"

"Bob, don't yell at me."

"Yell at you! Yell at you! You don't know what yelling is!"

And on it went, in that luxury motor home, their voices growing louder and more accusatory. And though Alan loved his father deeply, he was the one he always hated when they quarreled.

The shouting back and forth gradually turned into silence, then the tension in the silence began to ease up when his father found his glasses when he reached under his seat, where they'd fallen. He apologized, several times, but Alan's mother stayed silent for a while. But then, looking out her window, she began remarking about the beauty of the bay they were crossing over, so blue and dazzling in the sun; and soon they were a family again.

My own mother and her new husband—a marriage that would last about five more months, ending in her second divorce—had rented a beach-front house (on pilings) for a couple of weeks in Sea Belle, on the New Jersey seashore. I was nineteen, a junior at Bucknell, and was spending the weekend with them before going back to my summer job moving things from one place to another in a large wholesale grocery warehouse. I didn't like the guy and wasn't all that happy about being there. But I was looking forward to seeing Alan and his folks, who'd said they would be visiting for a few hours before moving on.

I remember their large motor home pulling up in front of the house, and marveling that my uncle was driving one for the first time at his age. He represented to me all the security in the world, a little remote but solid, just as my aunt was all smiling warmth. I envied Alan his parents, though that didn't mean I wasn't crazy about my mother. Thin where my aunt was a little heavy, she sold dresses at a luxury department store, loved to laugh, was the first on the dance floor at weddings, and thought I could do no wrong. I just wished she had better taste in men, including my father, who was living somewhere or other.

Alan had a nice smile, and we slapped each other's hand hello. In a way, he was still a kid to me at fifteen; it wasn't easy to let go of the memory of once making sure he held my hand when he crossed a street. He was thin and as tall as he would ever be, just as at his age I was already my present six-one.

After the usual hugging, they showed us through the motor home, something that only enhanced my feeling of their togetherness, and after lunch we went out to the beach. I remember walking single-file along the path through the high dune that almost hid the ocean from the street. Long tufts of grass speckled the dune and there was a partly buried line of wire-strung palings along both sides of the path.

The beach was fairly crowded; a lifeguard stand was about a half-block away. A few people waved to us as we came out. We set up the chairs we'd been carrying and put up a large beach umbrella, though no one sat under it.

As I remember, I was talking to Alan about a soccer game he'd been in when another couple, the Devlins, who were friends of my mother from home and were staying nearby, walked over to say hello. He was a rather short, bald-headed man, his wife a homely woman, gaunt-faced and with a slightly hooked nose and red-tinted hair. They set up their chairs to sit for "just a few minutes," as Mrs. Devlin said.

It was shortly after this that my aunt said, "Alan, let me put some sunblock on you." She was leaning forward in her chair, holding out the bottle toward him.

"Not right now."

"The sun's very strong, you're going to get burned."

"I said I will, not just now." He was obviously annoyed.

"I'm telling you," she warned gently.

He turned away and looked down the beach. He was obviously embarrassed, a teenager's embarrassment, that she was still holding out the bottle when he'd said no; I could just see him thinking, God, didn't she understand no? The ocean was a deep green with high breakers that were bringing in some seaweed; the sand had a black fringe near the water's edge. People were jumping up and down in the waves, or diving under them, or streaking on rafts to the beach. I noticed him watching a couple of girls in bikinis talking up to the two lifeguards on the stand; noticed it because I was looking there too.

"Alan," Mrs. Devlin suddenly directed a question at him, "are you driving yet?"

"No," his mother answered for him, "he's got a year to go."

"Oh my, just wait till he's sixteen."

"Oh I can't wait for that scene," my aunt said, and because she and the others were smiling, Alan apparently felt he had to smile too, though he was obviously embarrassed.

"How are the girls treating you?" Mr. Devlin asked him.

He shrugged and with this his father said, "The goils? I don't think he's going out with goils yet."

It wasn't the first time Alan had heard him refer to girls in this way when it had something to do with him. He didn't know why but it was as though his father had a problem not just with the word but with the idea of him with girls. Alan looked away, hoping that would deflect conversation from him, and it did. But soon he was looking back. He looked at Mrs. Devlin, who was turned the other way, talking with his mother. She had on a green one-piece bathing suit, a wide-brimmed straw hat, and sunglasses that had bits of colored shell on the frames. Homely though she was, she was well built, with long shapely legs.

He turned away when she looked back.

He asked me if I wanted to go in the water and I thought about it and then shook my head. He stood up, thinking, as he would recall it, that if his mother said anything like be careful, which wouldn't have bothered him any other time, he would have broken, red-faced, into a run. But she didn't. He had always been a good swimmer and the water was just cold enough for him. He dove under a wave and then another, and then swam beyond where they were breaking and continued parallel to the beach. When he came out he shook away the towel my aunt handed him and started to sit down but then remained standing.

Actually he was telling himself to sit down, just sit down, but even though it had become an outright plea now he still remained standing. And then he said, "I'll be right back, I want to get something from the car."

My mother said, "You want the bathroom, use the house. There are two."

"No, I want to get something."

His father must have turned off the air conditioning, so the heat of the motor home blasted him as he opened the door, but he didn't put it back on, telling himself he would just change into dry trunks and go out again. He locked the door and changed, but instead of leaving he sat down on the sofa. Behind his closed eyes he sought a face, a body. He thought of the two girls at the lifeguard stand, of some movie actresses, of some centerfolds and of bra and panty ads, and then, almost reluctantly, of Mrs. Devlin.

He tried to fight against it, knowing he would despise himself, already half despising himself. But gradually that homely face took on a kind of smile it didn't have in real life.

Give it to Mrs. Devlin, she was saying, please honey, give it to Mrs. Devlin.

From what I was to learn, they stopped at a couple of places in Maine, then headed up to the tip of Cape Cod, to Provincetown. They thought they might stay there at least one night but it felt too crowded and they started to head back. But soon my uncle began exploring and pulled into a wide dirt lane that led through thick woods to the top of a high dune overlooking an empty beach and the ocean.

My aunt said, "Are we allowed to stay here?"

"I don't know," my uncle said. "I don't see why not."

"Did you know when you turned off it would lead to the ocean?"

"I thought it might."

"Do you have any idea where we are?"

"Well, I saw a sign."

They were, he said, on the outskirts of South Minton.

Chapter Four

Alan got up about eleven the next morning, which was late for him, and was a little surprised that his parents were just getting up too. He stepped outside, into a bright clear day, and walked to the edge of the dune: The beach was empty as far as he could see to either side. After breakfast the three of them half-slid, half-walked down the dune, carrying a blanket and a couple of small sand chairs. They had some paperbacks and a transistor radio that they didn't turn on. Alan sat on the blanket, a book in hand. He was tan by now, didn't need sunblock anymore.

He had recently gotten into Salinger, and one of the books he'd brought along was a collection of his short stories. But he found it hard to concentrate and put it down. He looked at the ocean, which was fairly calm that day. As he stared at it his thoughts began drifting and then went back in time and settled on Mrs. Devlin. How, he asked himself for the dozenth time, could he have thought of that with *her*? And yet remembering what his mind had done to those legs and even that hooked nose and terrible red hair gave him an answer that he could feel all over again. He got up and said he was going in the water.

"Hey, just remember," his mother said, "there's no lifeguard around here."

He nodded, walking away before his father might decide to explain to him again about riptides, how if you got caught in one you shouldn't try to fight it but swim parallel to the beach until you could swim in. But he didn't go too far out, just enough past the waves where he could swim easily. When he came back he said he was going for a run. This, they expected: He loved running, had run as far as twenty miles a few times, though he knew he could run much farther. He took off slowly along the surf. The woods stretched on above the dunes to his left; he couldn't see a house.

After about half a mile he took another swim, this time a quick one, and then, because the sun was so bright and he wasn't wearing sunglasses, he decided to run back through the woods if possible. He didn't know if there was any kind of trail back there or if his bare feet could take it. But he liked the idea of testing and toughening his feet.

He climbed up the dune at a spot where there was an opening in the woods. He walked in about fifty feet and found a sandy trail through the trees, but it went in the opposite direction from where they were parked. He started walking along it, then began jogging again, slowly, taking in the silence and feel of the woods, which he'd always associated with Indians ever since he was a kid. In fact he used to daydream as a kid about being an Indian boy, in a loincloth or naked and running free.

He ran a short distance and then stopped at a lane that went to his right to the beach. He was about to turn back when he saw a girl of about twelve standing looking at him and then up at the trees and then back to him. Her skin was light brown, and she had long glistening black hair. She was wearing a two-piece bathing suit, the halter flat.

He said, "Do you want something?"

Without answering she pointed to a tree. He saw a red kite caught on one of the lower limbs.

"I'll see if I can get it for you."

He had to go a few yards back on the lane and then went in among the trees. The kite was on a thin limb that grew, twisted, toward the ground but it was a little beyond his reach. He jumped up and after a couple of tries caught the limb in his hand and bent it down. Stretching out his arm he grabbed hold of the kite and shook it free from the branch and it floated down. He noticed now that it was torn. When he started to walk to the lane with it, he saw that she'd come in a few feet and was standing there, looking at him.

"You know," he said, "it really wasn't worth the trouble. It's no good anyway, it's got," and he used a word that he only wished he could take back, "a hole in it. Can you see the hole?"

She didn't answer. She kept looking at him.

"It's got a hole in it," he repeated.

He found himself staring back at her. She was such

a pretty thing, her large eyes as black as her hair. Her bathing suit hugged her firm slender body.

Suddenly he wanted to say that word again.

"Do you know what a hole is?"

She still didn't answer.

He told himself to get out of there, to run from there, but instead he kneeled down and put his forefinger on her groin. She gave a quick gasp. But she didn't move, as if frozen. He started to stand up, heart galloping, still begging himself to run, run, to get away from this girl and these silent trees and back into the sun, but instead he stooped down again and hooked his finger under the swimsuit at her legs, to feel her skin.

"Stop," she shouted. "Stop it!"

She started to pull back, then began to cry. A cry that was like a fire alarm in his brain.

"Don't," he pleaded, jumping up. "Don't cry, please don't cry. You can go. I'm sorry, you can go."

She whirled and started to run, still crying. Terrified, he grabbed her shoulder. "Don't tell—please don't tell."

"Let me go! Let me go!"

"Listen to me. Please."

She started to shake free and he grabbed her again, this time hooking his arm around her throat, and her cry was cut off. He began dragging her deeper among the trees and threw her down. He stared at her, lying motionless face down. He stood there for several moments, but she still didn't move. A part of him wanted to kneel down to feel for breath, but instead he began to run. He ran deep into the trees, ran stumbling, soon suddenly lost, not knowing in which direction was his home—the motor home was *home*—then running just to keep running.

He was sure he had killed her.

Chapter Five

He kept running in panic, this way, that. At one point the woods opened to another lane and he took it but it led to the beach and he didn't want to be seen on the beach; it was as though people were already looking for him, would point and yell and come racing after him. He ran back into the woods again but couldn't find the narrow trail he'd been on, and he made his way around trees, jumping over fallen limbs, heading in first one direction and then the other. And then he saw sunlight ahead between the trees. It was another lane to the beach, and this one was where the motor home was parked.

He ran inside and closed and locked the door. He almost crumpled to the floor but stood there trembling violently, his arms around his chest. He was still trembling as he lowered himself to a crouch, then covered his face with his hands, fingers digging into his skin. *Oh God, oh God, what did I do?*

The police would come here, they would grab him, they would put him in handcuffs, they would take him away, everything was over! And Mom and Dad—oh God, Mom and Dad!

Why hadn't he just run from her? Why had he stayed? And why *that*?

He began to cry. He cried until he couldn't any more, and then out of sheer weakness he dropped across the sofa, his face in his arms.

He leaped up, hearing a rattling of the door.

The police?

The police!

But he slowly opened the door to his mother. She was looking at him in anger.

"Why didn't you come back to us? You had us worried!"

"I-I'm sorry."

"Sorry. Sorry. That was the dumbest thing. You had us scared. And why was this door locked?"

"I don't know. I just got tired."

His father came in then. "What's going on here?"

"He was here sleeping all this time."

My uncle addressed him. "You should have come back. You had your mother worried."

"Like you weren't," my aunt said to him. And then a look of dismay crossed her face. "Alan, you're bleeding on the floor. What happened to your feet?"

He sat down and looked at the bottom of his feet. One of them had a small cut. He hadn't even felt any pain.

"Where were you?" his mother demanded.

"I guess…in the woods." He didn't even want to say that; didn't want to place himself anywhere.

"You guess? You guess? What do you mean you guess?"

"I was in the woods, I was running in the woods." From the way they were looking at him he was sure they knew he had done something terrible, something beyond belief.

"Alan, don't raise your voice at me. That was the dumbest thing. Running in the woods. Bob," she said, turning to my uncle, "bring me a wet washcloth. And the Neosporin or Polysporin, I don't know which I brought. And a Band-Aid."

But all my cousin was thinking now was: *Let's get away from here! Drive away! Oh hurry, hurry!*

They did leave, an hour and a half later, but his father drove only about a mile down the road, to an intersection where a sign—with an arrow pointing to the right—read: SOUTH MINTON.

"Let's take a look at the town," he said.

"No," Alan cried out, "let's go on, I'm tired!"

"What's the matter?" his mother asked.

"I'm just tired."

"Tired?" his father repeated, with a look over his shoulder at him. "What're you so tired from?"

"I don't know." He was desperate.

"Look, you're not making sense. Go back to sleep if you want to. I just want to see the place." And he turned in the arrow's direction.

Alan almost dropped to the floor, to try to hide from the town. He couldn't think and was this close to bursting out in tears and saying something about the girl, but instead he remembered the cut on his foot and said, "My foot is bothering me."

"Oh it'll be fine," his mother said, "with the antibiotic and the Band-Aid."

"It should teach you not to run barefoot where you shouldn't," his father said. Then, "Hey, this is a very nice town."

But Alan didn't look. He went back to the sofa and lay across it, below the windows, his arms across his eyes and his eyes squeezed tight, terrified that he would hear sirens coming closer behind them. Then even after they drove from the town about a half hour later, it was miles before he dared peek out a window, still half-expecting to see police cars pulling alongside of them.

Please God, he kept praying silently, *help me, please dear Jesus help me.*

But at some point he stopped. For he began picturing that girl on Jesus's lap and him holding her tight and rocking back and forth. And for the first time, his hands on either side of his head, he stopped thinking only of himself.

Oh little girl I'm sorry, I'm sorry!

Just as, earlier, there had been times when he wished the trip was already over, times when he didn't feel like being closed in with his parents anymore, now he found himself wishing it would last forever. The motor home had become a fortress for him. Even when hundreds of miles away from South Minton, he dreaded stepping out of the trailer to go on a beach or have dinner or sightsee. And he was afraid of the end of the trip, was terrified of what he would find at home: a police car parked at the curb.

To his dismay his father broke the trip off after only another five days: Something had come up and he had to get back to the office. But as they turned into their street and headed toward their house, Alan almost let out a sob of relief. No police car was waiting. Only the quiet, cool brightness of the house.

Chapter Six

As Alan drove on to South Minton, he found himself thinking that the weather was like the workings of his own head in that it didn't seem to know what to do. He had driven only about fifteen miles from the service station when it began snowing again: Gray bulbous clouds had moved in swiftly and covered the sky. It was a heavy snow this time but a wet one, the kind his wipers cleared away easily.

After about forty more miles he pulled into a truck stop for lunch, the only decent-looking place to eat for the past several miles. Actually he wasn't hungry at all; this was, he was aware at the time, a way of slowing up the ride, of giving himself more of a chance to really decide, perhaps to change his mind.

The parking lot held a scattering of eighteen-wheelers. For a few moments their large cabs, most of them with an overhead bunk, seemed to hold a kind of security; it gave him something of the feeling he'd had as a small kid when, while looking at certain picture books, he would envy the squirrels and rabbits the warmth and coziness of their little homes in tree trunks.

Sitting at one of two fairly crowded semi-circular counters, he ordered a grilled cheese sandwich and a cup of coffee. While he was waiting, the man next to him, a big fellow, a driver, glanced over from his platter of veal and French fries. "You won't believe this but I've only had one heartburn in my life."

Alan was hardly in a mood to talk. But he said, trying hard to be polite, "Really. You're lucky."

"And I've never gotten rid of it," he grinned.

"Well, you got me."

"Sorry, but that was just pulled on me."

The fellow began telling him how he drove all over the country, almost always with another guy, though not this time, and it was really a good life for the most part. Then soon after the man returned to his meal, he looked over at the next counter where another man, a woman and a boy of about four had just sat down.

"Stu," he called. "Marie."

"Hey there," Stu called back, and Marie, a husky woman, gave him a big smile.

"I forget the little fellow's name," he apologized.

"Billy," she said.

"Hi, Billy, how are you?" Then, after not even getting a look from the boy, he said to them, "Where you heading?"

"Albuquerque," the man answered, "You?"

"Detroit, then Chicago."

Soon afterward he said to Alan in a low voice, "They own their own rig. She started sharing the driving when they got married, and they've been taking the kid since he was born."

Alan looked at them, the father holding a menu to his face, the mother talking to the boy who was playing with a little fire engine on the counter.

Finished with lunch, Alan stalled a little more, began looking around the place. It had just about everything an overnight trucker would need, including a food and toiletries market and, in the back, showers and some bunks. But there was no way of stalling any more, and he went out to his car and pulled out on the road fast, only to slow to the speed limit almost immediately. He always tried to go under the speed limit, which used to give his friends a big laugh. But he didn't ever want to be stopped by a cop.

Soon his thoughts began drifting back to the couple and their son at the counter. How he envied them having each other.

A wife, a family—if he didn't turn back he could be giving up even a hope of that, forever.

He couldn't remember exactly when he began thinking that he might not have killed her. But it had to have started after the first few months, when not only didn't the police show up but he saw nothing in the news about any crime in or around South Minton. Still, he was always anxious when he read or watched the news and, much later, when he watched, whenever he dared to, one TV show in particular about unsolved crimes, always wondering with a fast-beating heart would her face appear, and then afterward feeling great waves of relief when it didn't.

"What're you watching that junk for?" his mother asked him once.

He said something quickly like, "It's interesting." But it was as if he'd been caught at something.

Gradually, whenever he summoned up the courage to think back and try to pick apart that horror, he became almost sure that he couldn't have killed her, that his arm had never been hooked that tight around her neck. In fact, as he'd pulled her back among the trees, he'd loosened his grip, and his other hand had taken hold of her swimsuit strap and shoulder. And so he might have only stunned her or knocked her unconscious when he threw her to the ground.

The day before he'd had to go back to school after the trip—he was a junior in high school—his father came into his room, where he was trying to win a game of chess against the computer. He looked so solemn that Alan's heart leaped. His father sat down on a chair facing him.

"Alan, I want to talk to you about something. And I hope it doesn't get you angry."

Alan just stared at him.

"I should have talked to you about this before but I was really afraid you'd get angry. And I didn't think you needed it. In fact I still don't. But your mother and I, you know, feel I should. It's about drugs."

Alan almost sighed.

"I'm sure you're not involved in anything like that," his father hurried on, "but I just wanted to say it. It's more, you know, it's more for me than you." And he smiled, waiting for Alan to say something.

"I haven't taken any drugs," he said, "and I don't intend to."

"Look," his father smiled, and Alan could feel his relief, "I said I didn't think you did, I was positive of it, but—you know—right?"

Alan nodded.

"Good." He stood up. "Well, you sleep well."

Alan looked at the door as he closed it. And thought with a silent cry: *Oh Dad! Oh Daddy!*

Indeed, not only was he was never to smoke pot, he never drank alcohol until he was in his twenties, and then barely at all. But this had nothing to do with anything his father had said. He was afraid if he got high he might blurt out his crime.

He'd been a good student up until that terrible summer. In fact he was skipped ahead a class in elementary school, which put him in his friend Will Jansen's grade; the day he found out was the most joyous day of his boyhood. But although he always tried hard, his marks fell after that summer. Not that he was ever a *bad* student, but he hovered just below the excellent ones, where he was sure he actually belonged. And while he fought it, he was still obsessed with sex, though he was afraid of girls. He never went to a dance in high school or even to his senior prom, wriggling out of it when a girl he secretly loved put her leg around his in one of their classes and, leaning sideways toward him, whispered would he take her to it.

He didn't know if this had any part in it but he couldn't shake the fear that he would hurt—kill?—another girl.

He didn't even bother applying to Harvard, where his father had gone, but he was accepted by several colleges, including Penn State, where he went. He had no idea what he wanted to be and so had no major the first couple of years; he couldn't see himself as a lawyer anymore, certainly not a criminal lawyer: Saving the innocent had turned in his mind into freeing the guilty. All he knew was that he wanted to do "good," to make up for his sins, his crime; do something as amorphous and juvenile as saving the world.

He made friends at State and began dating a little. One of the first girls he took out was Sarah, a freshman like him. She had a bright face and short blond hair, and her own car. Their first date, they began kissing in the front seat in some dark park, and he loved kissing her, his hands under her hair at the back of her head. And when he started to open her blouse and their legs got entangled with the steering wheel, she said, "In back. Can we?"

And he went back there with her and they kissed again and he held her breasts, but when she waited for him, skirt high on her white thighs and legs apart, he suddenly realized in shock that he had nothing there. And it was later, in his room, that he thought, face in his hands, that this was to be his punishment.

Chapter Seven

Unlike Alan, I used to smoke more than an occasional joint, though I stopped after college, often had too many beers, dated girls without commitment. I also did well enough in college to get into law school, where I stayed just one year. I had met a man who said he'd been a freelance writer for a couple of true detective magazines for years but was giving it up for health reasons. For a long time I'd had what I thought was a fantasy of being a writer, and I took a chance and went to New York to meet the editor, Sam Haggerty, a white-haired man in his sixties, a chain-smoker who ran two magazines, *Detective Eye* and *Crime Central*, in a small office with one other editor and an artist.

I'm sure he looked at my college writing samples with a skeptical eye, but there must have been something about them and me he liked. He explained to me the types of articles he wanted and was honest enough to say that the heyday of these magazines was long over. Then he tried me out on a murder in Philadelphia, which involved my interviewing a couple of detectives. I wrote it well enough that I was promised other assignments—and that was the end of law school. In the following years I not only covered crimes for him in New Jersey, Maryland and Delaware but I also contributed to some national magazines and published four books on true crime.

I had a girlfriend once who asked me if all this writing about crime didn't keep me up at night. I said no, which was true. Actually the only crimes that really affected me, and affected me deeply, were those against children. I'd always been against the death penalty, but that was the one exception: I wanted those monsters dead.

Alan finally did decide to go to law school, for pretty much the same reason I did: It wasn't that he wanted to be a lawyer but he saw it as a good background for whatever he eventually decided to do. Again he didn't go to the school, Yale, his father did—he didn't even apply, to his father's dismay. My uncle was sure he could have gotten in as the son of an alumnus, which is what Alan would have always felt and didn't want. The two law schools he did apply to accepted him and he chose Temple, in Philly, and took a studio apartment downtown.

It was in his second year that he got a call there from his mother, in a voice that told him, with just her first word, "Alan," that something was wrong. His father had died at his desk in his office, probably, as we were to learn later, of an aortic aneurysm.

The viewing was the first I'd seen Alan and my aunt in several months. I went up to my aunt first, who smiled sadly at me through the several people who were around her. Then she put her arms around me, and when I said something about him being a wonderful man she said, "Colin, everyone loved him. He was such a good person." Then, referring to the swift passing of their years together, "It was only like a walk around the block." When I went over to Alan, we held each other too, briefly, and after I said the usual things, I remember him saying, "I know how you felt about him." And I also remember thinking: No, you don't. For as I looked at my uncle lying there, face strong even in death, one of the many thoughts I had, strangely enough—but perhaps not—was of him at the wheel of that motor home as he was about to drive off: all that I would have wanted!

His funeral was the first time I'd been in church in years—and Alan's first since before South Minton. He hadn't been able to face going and his parents had eventually stopped pushing him. Now, as he was to tell me, he felt as though God and all of the angels and half the dead were looking down at him.

As he kept staring at the coffin, one thought began running through his mind: *Dad, what were your problems that I will never know about—just as you never knew mine?* And then at the cemetery, where the sun even came out after a morning of gray drizzle, another thought raced through him: *Now that he's with the dead, perhaps even with that little girl, he knows what I have done.*

Alan called me on his cell phone a couple of weeks after the funeral. I had told him that I'd moved into a new apartment and he said he was driving through the neighborhood, did I mind if he stopped by.

I said, "Are you kidding? Of course I mind."

He laughed. "I'm going to cry."

"In that case, hurry."

I had moved to a much larger apartment, this one on the second floor of an artsy gift shop in the Chestnut Hill section of the city. It was early April and still quite chilly, but he was wearing only a thin tan sweater, chinos and Docksiders. He had nice things to say about the place, the prints on the walls, the fireplace, the two walls lined with books, and after a while said, "You must work very closely with the police."

"Oh yeah. That's part of it."

"Do you get real friendly with them?"

"Just with a couple of them. The rest I pretty much just know."

"Tell me, how do you keep up to date on crimes?"

"Well, I subscribe to a number of papers. I hear from the editors. And there's always TV."

As I look back on it, I am sure he wanted to ask a lot more questions, that he had stopped by only for that, but then had become afraid to. Yet even if he had, I don't think there is any way I would have looked on it as suspicious. I had such a special feeling for him. He would always be my kid cousin but even more than that, as I've said, like my kid brother. I would always remember the first time I saw him in my aunt's arms, and wanting to hold him and then being allowed to touch his little arms. And the feeling I was to have in those early years that I was someone who should look after him and protect him. I was delighted that he'd grown up to be such a clean-cut guy, good looking and soft spoken, with a self-deprecating sense of humor. And I was proud that he was with a prestigious law firm.

He had joined a firm where he wouldn't have to do any litigation; he had no taste for trials. For a while he did tax law, then began specializing in estate work, which would one day lead to a different career for him. He had a social life, though he rarely went with any girl more than twice, maybe three times. He had a few good friends, guys, all of whom, from their conversations, assumed he was the lover they professed to be. And though he often thought of going to a psychiatrist, once to the point of even making an appointment, that road was closed: He could never reveal what haunted him.

Then one day he got sick.

He was taking his twice-a-week run, a five miler, and was into the second mile when he felt a hollowness and an aching in his chest. He stopped and bent over, his hands on his knees, but it wouldn't pass. When he straightened up he felt a little better and he started walking back. But it turned out that he needed a gall-bladder operation.

And though he argued against it and even went for a second opinion, he had to have general anesthesia.

He remembered thinking, as he was being wheeled into the operating room, that he might wake up to police staring down at him.

"Which little girl? Where was this? When?"

But he woke to a recovery room nurse's smiling face. "Come on now. It's all over. Come on."

He was in the hospital four days longer than expected because he developed a fever. And it was on the second morning that he met Anna—ANNA PRESIAC, LPN, her nametag read. She was about five-four, slender and nicely built, with pulled-back blond hair and pale skin. She looked to be about twenty-three. One of the first things he noticed about her as she came into the room was her smile; it was so warm. And so were her eyes. And so, as it turned out, was everything about her.

"You look so much better than yesterday," she greeted him.

"Oh? Did I see you yesterday?"

"No, but I saw you. You were asleep."

All the nurses he had were kind but there was something special about Anna, even in her touch when she squeezed his wrist with a smile while attending him. Her presence seemed to bring a glow to the room—certainly it brightened him. She would often look in even when he didn't ring for a nurse.

"You look grouchy," she said one time.

"Me? Grouchy? Are you sure you have the right patient?"

She laughed. "Yes, I have the right patient. You were frowning down to here." And she made a face.

"Oh, then I must have a very pretty smile."

She considered this. "Oh. Well, thank you."

He looked forward to seeing her again, but another

nurse replaced her that afternoon. Nor did she show up the next day. He asked one of the nurses where she was.

"Oh, her? She left. She quit."

"Quit?" He felt a jolt of dismay. "Just like that?"

"As far as I know."

He looked at the nurse. Then it just came out of him: "Do you know if she's married?"

"She isn't, no." Then she looked at him rather strangely, with a slight shake of her head in warning. "Ooo, no, no. This isn't the first place she's quit. I'll deny it if you repeat it, but that girl," and she waved her hand in front of her face, "is a bit of a nutcase. Wifty."

Chapter Eight

He couldn't shake Anna from his mind. He'd never dated anyone as pretty—as beautiful. And it wasn't just her looks that pulled at him, but her great warmth and a sense she projected that nothing human could disturb her. He had heard all the stories about guys falling in love with their nurses, and now after his first stay in a hospital he knew why. And yet he didn't want to believe that this was anything ordinary.

He tried dialing Information for the city and suburbs but there was no listing for her name. He then tried locating her through the Internet but here, too, he came up with nothing. And then, though he was certain it would be useless, he did what he should have done right away, he called the hospital's nursing office.

"Anna Presiac?" a woman repeated. "I'm sorry, she doesn't work here any more."

"I understand that. I'm an old friend of hers"—he didn't want to say "former patient"—"and I'm trying to locate her. I was wondering if there's any way you could help me."

"I'm sorry, we don't give out any phone numbers or addresses for employees or former employees."

"I appreciate that. But what if I give you my phone

number, could someone get in touch with her and ask her to call me?"

"I'm sorry, we're all quite busy."

"Just one call to her? That's all I ask."

"Look, I don't even know if she's still at the address we have for her." Then, after a long pause and with obvious reluctance, "What's your name and phone number?"

When he didn't hear from Anna in the next two days he was sure they hadn't even passed on his number. On the third day, however, he came home and one of the messages on his answering machine was, "This is Anna Presiac. You tried to reach me. Who are you?" And that was it. She didn't leave a phone number where he could call her.

He thought of what that nurse had said of her—a nutcase, wifty. And he assumed that he'd now heard the last of her. But it was about a week later that he answered the phone to hear: "Mr. Benning? Alan Benning?"

He knew instantly who it was. "That's right. Hi."

"This is Anna Presiac," she went on. "You asked me to call you. Forgive me but I can't place the name. Who are you?"

"I was one of your patients. Gall-bladder surgery. But it's no wonder you don't remember me. You were my nurse only for a day—actually maybe two. You said I was asleep the first time you saw me."

She paused to think. Then, with a new brightness to her voice, "Oh yes. Yes. I think I remember."

"The guy with the two noses."

She laughed. "Oh now I definitely remember. How are you?"

"Good. Very good." He felt so lighthearted all at once. "I want you to know I was very disappointed to hear that you left."

"Oh that was something I just had to do. But it's nice to hear. I should have said goodbye but I didn't want to cause any fuss."

"I know I would have refused all food and drink."

She laughed again. "That would have been very noble of you."

"Really? Did you ever eat that food?"

"Oh it wasn't that bad, was it?"

"No, it was almost okay. Look, am I terribly nosy if I ask if you have another job?"

"You're not nosy at all. The answer is that I didn't when I left but I do now."

"Well, I want to wish you good luck. You're an absolutely marvelous nurse, which I'm sure adds up to an absolutely marvelous person."

"Well, thank you." He felt she was smiling. "And how about yourself? You feel okay? Any problems afterward?"

"None." And then it just came out, a burst of silliness: "Well, except I miss my gall bladder."

"Huh?"

"I'm sorry," he apologized, "I don't know where that came from. I just feel good."

"Well, that's nothing to apologize for. That's marvelous."

"Look," he said, "I guess you're wondering why I got in touch. Or maybe you have a perfectly good idea. Anyway, it's definitely not about hospital food. I'm wondering if I could see you."

There was silence, though he was sure she wasn't surprised. "I don't know. I really don't date patients."

"I'm not a patient anymore, remember?"

She laughed. Then, "I'm going to be blunt. Are you married?"

"Just to my work."

"Seriously, are you?" It was so obvious she'd been hit on by married guys.

"No. Seriously."

"Well…" She paused, thinking. "I can't tonight but how about meeting me tomorrow for a cup of coffee? There's a little cafe down the corner from my place called Lonergan's, they serve good coffee, tea, even little sandwiches."

Lonergan's was a small place, with bare wooden tables and chairs, and paintings and drawings by local artists on the walls. There was an oaken counter on one side of the air-conditioned room with urns behind it. He got there about ten minutes before she did. It was an exceptionally warm night for early spring, and she was wearing a white sleeveless blouse, jeans and sandals. He had on an polo shirt, tan slacks and moccasins.

They ordered two lattés, then began probing into each other's background. She told him she'd been born and raised in a small town, Tamaqua, in the anthracite coal region of the state.

"I'll bet," she said, "you don't even know what anthracite is."

"You'd lose. Hard coal."

"Which means what?"

"It's the kind when you throw it at someone, it hurts."

She laughed. "You are something. They say it burns a lot cleaner. Anyway, it was a big thing at one time. My grandfather and great-grandfather used to work the mines. But that day's long gone. My dad has a garage, which I mention," she smiled, "because you should see me in it. I love working on cars."

"You mean, you not only fix people, you fix cars, too?"

"Yep. And I love getting greasy."

"You amaze me. Are there any brothers or sisters in the picture?"

"Just a sister. Younger. And she's a real brat. And if you think I'm kidding, I'm not."

"Can I ask you something about nursing? Did you ever think of becoming an RN?"

"Yeah, but it would have taken longer and I wanted to get away and I needed to work as soon as possible. LPNs do many of the same things anyway."

"This is none of my business and you don't have to tell me, but why did you quit?"

"Oh, I just didn't like the way certain things were being done. I can put up with a lot, but when it affects patient care, no." She left it at that, then said with a big smile, "Did I tell you I got a new job? It's at a nursing home. A very nice one."

He looked at her and didn't say anything except, "Congratulations." Nothing about what he was thinking: How could that attract you? How could you bear it day after day? But it was not only with wonder but a deep feeling of admiration.

They stayed there until about eleven, then he walked with her down the block to the large graystone house, one of a row of identical houses, where she had an apartment. They went up the high front steps, where she unlocked the outer door and then turned to him and hugged him. He kissed her on the lips and she kissed back, but then straightened up. Her body language said: You're not to go inside this building.

He said, "I'll call you, okay?"

She nodded. "I'll shoot you if you don't."

"Promise?"

She laughed and leaned forward and kissed him quickly on the lips.

He was to remember, when things changed a little later, how good he'd felt as he drove to a convenience store near his apartment to pick up milk for the morning. The parking lot was surprisingly crowded for this hour and he stood parked, his left flasher on, waiting for a car near the front doors to back out. But then as it did, another car came fast down the drive and started pulling into the spot. The driver, a man in a sleeveless shirt, couldn't make it with one turn, though, and had to back out. Alan—like a stupid ass—jumped out of his car.

"Hey! You saw me waiting. You saw I was going to pull in."

The driver didn't even look at him.

"Why the hell don't you learn how to drive?" Even that stupid, stupid remark. But it was enough to bring the driver out of his car, a fellow about Alan's height and age but much heavier, his face on fire.

"Who the fuck do you think you are?" the man demanded.

"I was waiting here! You saw me waiting!"

"Well, go fuck yourself and wait."

"Oh go to hell."

He started to walk away from Alan, then turned and strode back, and after more shouting back and forth they were swinging at each other. A couple of minutes later, as they both stood there out of breath but with their fists still clenched, a police car pulled in, siren whining, in response to somebody's phone call.

The cop didn't take either of them in but several days later Alan got notice that he was to appear in Municipal Court: The other fellow was accusing him of attacking him. He was cleared, but in a sense it didn't matter. What mattered was that he had lost his temper in such a stupid way.

And it heightened the fear he'd had ever since the crime, that violence was a part of him.

Chapter Nine

He called Anna the day after the case was dismissed, early on a Saturday morning. It was several weeks since he'd seen her. Although he had been thinking about her, he'd been preoccupied with concern about going to court, and with work—and also with the strong feeling that he should not get too involved with anyone. But as he picked up the phone to call it was with anxiety that she might turn him down.

"Look," he apologized, "I'm sorry to be calling you this early"—it was about ten-thirty—"but I thought you might go out if you weren't working and I was hoping I could see you this evening."

"Oh, that sounds fine." No hesitancy or pretense because he hadn't called sooner.

"Great. What do you say about…" he was going to say "six." But he was looking toward the window, at the bright sun against it, and he said, "I'm just wondering. It looks like such a beautiful day I wonder if I could take you out for the day."

"Really? That sounds nice. I'd love it."

He picked her up about noon. She was wearing white slacks, a pink blouse and a baseball cap, and was holding, along with a light sweater over her arm, sunglasses.

"Take your pick," he said. "Out to Bucks County? Amish country? Peru? Or none of the above."

"Oh Peru, of course."

"Then I'll have to fill up the tank first."

They both laughed, and then she said, "I have an idea. Are your dates allowed to have ideas?"

"Not really. What?"

"How about a nice ride to Jersey? A beach?"

He felt a slight sagging around his heart. He hadn't been to any seashore since that summer; had avoided them as though all of the Atlantic Ocean and its beaches were part of that nightmare.

He said, "If you'd like. Sure."

"You don't sound too enthusiastic."

"No, that's fine."

"I mean it. Let's go someplace else. Bucks County— New Hope—great."

"No. I want the shore. Do you have a preference?"

"Well, have you ever been to Long Beach Island?"

"Yes. Once. Long ago." That had been when he was ten and they'd stayed at a motel for a few days. It was about sixty miles from the city.

"I was only there once myself and I loved it. It's so quiet compared to Atlantic City, Wildwood…"

He took the Benjamin Franklin Bridge over to New Jersey—Camden—and out past the city and finally to a two-lane road through country and woodland and then to another two-lane road that would lead to the island some thirty miles away.

Anna had started her new job the previous week

and, incredibly to him, was finding not only the satisfaction she'd hoped to find working with the sick and crippled aged, but something more—actual joy.

"It's hard to explain if someone doesn't feel it. These people, even the ones with Alzheimer's, have so much history to tell, if you just listen to them, have patience with them."

"You're remarkable, do you know that?"

"No, I'm not. Don't say that."

"Okay, I'll keep it to myself."

She looked at him and smiled and then reached over and squeezed his hand on the wheel.

They were approaching a causeway now that led over the bay to the island. And at the first sight of it, he felt a quick tightening in his chest and a rush of horrendous memories. This was so much like the approach to Sea Belle that it was as if Mrs. Devlin, dead now some five years, would be waiting for him there; and everything else that had followed seemed to be waiting there too.

The bay at that time had been alive with boats. Only two or three were out on its vastness now.

The road off the causeway ended at a traffic circle; they could go right or left on the street that cut through the narrow island. He turned left, having the vague memory that right was much busier.

Many of the shops still hadn't opened for the summer, and there were only a few cars on the street and just a handful of people on the sidewalks. He opened a window; the air seemed so clean, held the smell of the ocean. He could feel his tension easing away. Huge houses, many of them mansions, had replaced what he remembered as cottages here. But somehow, despite that, there was still a feeling to the place of vast sandy emptiness.

He parked near the end of the island, in view of the lighthouse there. Anna immediately took off her sandals and started to open her door, then seemed surprised that he was still sitting there.

"Don't you want to go out on the beach?"

"Yes. Sure." But he almost had to force himself to take off his Docksiders.

She was waiting for him in front of the car, her hand out to him. They walked hand in hand along a narrow path to the beach, and then far out on the wide beach toward the ocean. There was no other person around. In the distance an empty lifeguard stand lay on its back, like a gigantic insect.

They sat down on the sand. His heart had begun pounding and just wouldn't stop.

South Minton was over three hundred miles away, and yet it was as if that part of the ocean was bleeding into here.

"What're you doing?" she asked.

He almost wasn't aware that the fingers of his right hand had been digging hard into the sand. He had dug deep, reaching damp sand.

"Just trying to reach China," he said.

"You used to do that too?"

He managed a smile. "I'm still doing it."

She leaned against him and put her arm around him. He put his around her and squeezed her to him.

"Hey," she said after a few moments, "I can't breathe."

"Oh, I'm sorry." He released her immediately.

"No, no. I forgot to tell you I love not breathing."

They laughed. "You are something," he said, looking at her. He touched her right cheek with his fingertips. She turned just enough to kiss his palm.

He suddenly wanted to cry out Oh Anna! But he was even afraid to say her name, as if that would bring out more.

"You look like you're thinking," she said.

"Me? Just how happy I am to be with you."

She turned to him and they kissed. He felt that if he made them both naked and he lay with her here, everything would be perfect; he had no fear with her, only great need and desire. He touched her breasts and she pressed herself into his palms, kissing him hard. He started to unbutton her blouse on that wide empty beach but after a moment or two she shook her head.

"Please. Let's not here."

"I'm sorry."

"No. No, not that. Don't be sorry. Just not here."

After a while they drove to the other end of the island, and later had dinner at a restaurant on the causeway whose long bar was filled largely with construction workers. On the drive back she reached out and placed her hand on his knee, and whenever he glanced at her she would be looking at him, smiling. It was only as they approached the city that her mood seemed to change. Then, staring straight ahead, she said, "Can I tell you something? It's something I heard yesterday that has me upset."

"Of course."

"It's about my sister. She's pregnant. And she's only a kid herself. Just fifteen."

He didn't say anything right away. "What about the father?"

"He's a kid too. In fact she doesn't even want to see him anymore. And my father, he's so upset. Oh is he mad."

"How's your mother handling it?"

"Upset. Very upset. But—" She stopped. He said nothing, and then after a few moments she went on. "But she should be the last one to say anything. She had me when she was sixteen."

"With your father?" Anna was so open that he felt free to ask.

She nodded. "Yeah. That's why they got married, at least when they did. So, he's not one to talk either."

She became quiet again, and he drove on in silence. Then when he looked over at her she was looking at him. She said, "Are you upset with me?"

"Upset with you? Why?"

"Because of what I told you."

"Now why would I be upset with you over that?"

"I don't know. Because you might think I have a crazy family. I was just wondering."

"Oh no." And he reached over and took her hand. She squeezed it and held it to her lips.

Her apartment was on the second floor. He was feeling a rush of anxiety now, had first begun feeling it long before he turned into her street. Still, he led her over to the sofa and put his arms around her and kissed her. Her hands grew tight on his back. Lips open, they took in each other's breathing, and now his tongue was tangled with hers. Soon his hand moved to one of her breasts, held its fullness. But within a few seconds she sat up straight.

"Don't. Please don't."

He looked at her in surprise.

"Just don't. Please."

"I'm not."

"I can't," she said.

Then she lowered her head and began to cry. He watched her, then heard her say, as if to herself as much as to him: "I'm sorry. I'm sorry."

Chapter Ten

Driving away from the truck stop, Alan could still remember just looking at her and thinking again of those words "nutcase," "wifty."

Here he was, the thought went through him, scared of what lay ahead and yet a part of him was back there on that sofa, hearing her saying, "I'm sorry, I just don't feel well, please don't be mad." And then holding her but thinking this was the end of anything between them.

The snow was beginning to come down even harder now but he could see that the sky ahead was almost a summer blue. He began looking on the weather more and more as the proper crazy setting for what he was doing. And the questions he'd been trying to suppress ever since he started this drive were coming back like hammer blows.

What if I find out I did kill her? What then?

He almost closed his eyes to the splattering snow and the sweeping wipers.

But it can't be!

Then why are you going back there?

To clear his head of it once and for all, he kept telling himself. To be free in a way he hadn't been since that day.

But then why did a part of him want to turn the car around?

He was aware all at once of how slowly he'd begun to drive, as if to make this last hundred and fifty miles stretch on forever. And, even though reluctantly, he stepped a little harder on the gas.

Although he had told himself he would never call Anna again after that incident, his mind kept going back to her so many times during the next several days, even while he was writing a brief or having lunch with a client. She *was* a nutcase, she came from a family that seemed straight out of the old Ozarks, yet he couldn't shake her from his thoughts. Still, he didn't know if he would ever call her again. He would never get to find out: She called him the following week at his office, and from her voice it was as if nothing had gone wrong between them. She asked if he was free to come over for dinner that night. "Or any night."

"Oh, tonight's fine. I'd love to."

He got there at seven, with a bottle of merlot that he brought from his apartment. She was wearing a T-shirt and had an apron around her skirt. Her hair, which she often wore pulled back, was down. She smiled and took his hand and lifted her face for a kiss.

"Hon, make yourself comfortable. I just want to finish something."

The kitchen, with a small table to one side, was separated from the living room by a counter. He walked over to a photo that stood on a lamp table. It was her

LPN graduation picture, a head shot, showing her smiling and wearing a nurse's cap; the last time he'd seen a nurse wearing one was in an old movie. Nearby was a picture of her and her family, the four of them standing stiff, formal.

She'd made steaks and French fries and a salad, but felt it necessary to explain that she had come home at six and hadn't been able to make anything else.

"Are you kidding?" he said. "This is fine, more than fine. In fact you didn't have to make anything at all. We could have gone out."

"I wanted to make something for you."

After dinner, as he was walking to the sink with a couple of plates, she took them from him and set them down and, looking up at him, put her arms around him. They kissed each other hard, then softly, then hard again, their arms tight around each other. Then she took his hand and they walked into the bedroom. There she started to unbutton his shirt, then stopped as though her fingers had gotten too clumsy in her hurry. Instead she lifted her T-shirt over her head and then came close again in bra and skirt.

She looked up at him and kissed him as he unhooked her bra.

In bed he was aware of almost nothing but the feel and good smell of her and then almost miraculously the wondrous rhythm, slow at first and then faster, of their bodies.

"Oh Anna." Only the rhythm and just wanting to say her name.

"Yes, sweetheart, yes darling."

And then wanting only to hold her even tighter, longer, forever.

But it was only afterward, after they fell back and lay gently in each other's arms, their legs entangled, that he sensed something from her face that told him she hadn't really joined him at the end.

Chapter Eleven

They saw each other almost every night that week. And on Saturday she asked if he would like to drive her home to Tamaqua the next day, that she had a few things there she wanted to bring back to her apartment. He was happy to do it, was curious to meet her family.

When he went to pick her up she said, "Alan, don't be mad at me but I've got to stop at the nursing home. I forgot something completely. One of the patients is having a birthday and I bought something for her, and here I simply forgot."

"So why would I be mad at you?"

"I don't know. It'll be about an hour."

"Oh my, my life is ruined. The big thing is, am I invited?"

"Of course." She laughed and gave him a kiss.

The nursing home was a white, pillared building set on several acres of greenery near the outskirts of the city. He watched as Anna walked among the patients in the lounge, most of them in wheelchairs, sitting staring down at their laps. She paused to kiss a cheek here and there, or to urge a smile, or clasp a thin hand, or just to kneel and make a try at conversation. The birthday girl was a woman of ninety-one, and Anna's gift, among several others around the wheelchair, was a blouse, which she lifted from its box to the slight, quickly fading smile of the woman and the applause of a nurse and an attendant standing by.

Afterward, driving away, Alan said, "I don't know how you do it."

"How I do what?" She was frowning slightly as she turned to him.

"Everything you do. You have a magic touch."

"Ah." She leaned over and kissed his cheek.

He started noticing a change in her as they began driving through the old anthracite region, with its fields of green grass and occasional contrasting piles of black slag, the debris of long-abandoned mines. He wasn't going to mention anything to her, but she said, instead, "I'm nervous."

"Why? Because of my two noses?"

She laughed. "That would be all right. I'm thinking of my father. He can be very nice or else he can be tough."

"How does he respond to being slapped around?"

She laughed. "Oh you two will get along great."

Soon after they entered the town, she pointed to an auto repair shop, a CLOSED sign on the door, that had something of the look of a junkyard.

"That's my dad's place. We live a couple blocks away."

"You helped out here?"

"Sure, all through high school. I love it. In fact at

one time I only wanted to be on a Nascar crew."

"And what happened?"

"Dreams change." And she smiled, as if that were enough.

Her house was a two-story frame building with a small open porch. It was darkly Victorian inside; the furniture had a heavy look; a small crucifix hung in the dining room. For some reason, he had had the feeling that her mother might be grossly fat. She wasn't: She looked amazingly like Anna, with a nice warm smile. Her father was a husky man with thinning black hair, who looked expressionless except when he was frowning. He had a large tattoo on each forearm. Her sister, thin and with dyed orangey hair and large eyes that always seemed focused on Alan, wasn't showing her pregnancy yet and looked as if she wasn't concerned about a thing.

Her mother spoke almost incessantly, including about her two sisters whose husbands died years ago and her rich older brother, who was selling his paint manufacturing business. But for a long time Anna's father remained silent, though the few times Alan looked at him he was staring back.

It was shortly before dinner that her father began asking him questions, as though he'd been storing them up.

"Your mother and father living?"

"Just my mother. My father died."

"Did I hear you're not Catholic?"

"I'm not, no."

"You're what?"

"My religion? I was raised Lutheran."

"You believe in God." He said it as a statement.

"Yes."

He nodded thoughtfully. "Anna says you're a lawyer."

"Yes."

"They're not my favorite people, you know." He did smile slightly at this.

"Oh Dad," Anna spoke up.

"It's true." This time even that little smile was gone.

"Well, they're not always mine either," Alan said.

Her father seemed to like that. "Do you ever hunt?"

"No."

He pondered over this for a moment. "Did Anna ever tell you she's a natural at fixing cars?"

"Yes, she told me she loves it."

"Let me tell you something about this girl. She fixed a transmission—let's see, how old were you? Twelve?"

"You helped," she said. "You know you helped."

"Twelve. Fixed a transmission."

"Let's," her mother spoke up, "have dinner."

Dinner was roast beef, baked potatoes and string beans, with applesauce and iced tea. It was good, and they ate with a minimum of talk, with nothing at all that whole afternoon from the sister. Afterward, in the bathroom, Alan saw that the toilet seat was made of clear plastic, suspended inside which was a scattering of United States coins.

As he told Anna on the way home, "I think I sat on fifty dollars."

She seemed puzzled, then laughed. "Oh that."

"Don't laugh. That's part of your inheritance."

She laughed again; and looking at her, he became aware of how much he loved making her laugh.

A little while later it struck him that she hadn't brought anything back with her, the supposed reason she'd wanted to go there. It also struck him, even harder, that while he had been judging her family, they'd had no way of knowing the depths to which they'd have to go to even begin to judge him.

It was soon after this that his career began to take a different direction. He had made a good friend of Elsa Tomlinson, of the renowned Elsa and Jonathan Tomlinson Foundation, the national charity that provided grants in many fields including the arts and education. He had been called in by one of his firm's law partners to help her, a recent widow, reconstruct her will. And she had given him particular credit for it, to the point of having him do an increasing amount of the Foundation's legal work.

She called him at the office about a week after he'd met Anna's family.

"When can you have lunch with me?"

"Whenever you say."

"Wrong. You've got to sound busier if you're going to continue to work for me."

"You just reminded me. I'm tied up all this month."

"Good. One o'clock today at my club?"

She was a woman in her late sixties, with a narrow, handsome face, bright blue eyes, and pulled-back white hair. She and her husband had had no children. Although she never said anything to indicate it, certain movements of her hands seemed to indicate she missed the cigarettes she used to smoke.

"I'm having a martini," she said. "And you?"

"A scotch and soda."

"You don't like brands?"

Actually it didn't make any difference; he still didn't trust drinking. "A Dewar's will be fine."

With the waiter gone, she looked at him in a slightly arched way, as if examining him for the first time.

"I would like you to be on our board of directors."

"Oh?"

"Is that all you have to say?"

"No, but I'm gulping."

"Well, when you're finished tell me what you think."

"I'm delighted, of course. Thank you."

"Now stop gushing. And I will want you to come work for us. Not at this moment but quite soon, once I figure things out."

He said nothing, nor did she apparently expect him to.

"Are you a softie?" she asked. "In charity work you obviously have to be sort of a softie."

"I think I am."

"But you also have to be something else. If things work out the way I want them to, you might be the object of some jealousy. Can you also be a killer?"

He didn't answer. Her words came as kind of a shock.

"You can't?" She tilted her head.

"Yes," he said, "I can be a killer."

Chapter Twelve

As for me, I had gotten married a couple of months before Alan was tapped for the board of directors. My wife, Patty, was someone I'd been seeing for about a year. She was a librarian, a gently attractive and wise young woman of twenty-six. I'd first met her at the branch library she ran, where I'd gone to give a talk to one of their book groups, and I almost immediately stopped dating anyone else. She had met Alan once, for maybe a half hour, so perhaps it hadn't been long enough for her to sense something about him the way she did at our wedding, where as I've mentioned he was my best man.

It was a small wedding, which was what both of us wanted, with about twenty-five people, held at a chapel and culminating in a quiet side room of a fine restaurant near the suburbs. Alan looked fine to me, smiling, talking to people, and telling some jokes about me as he stood up from his table and gave a toast to us. So it came as a surprise to me when Patty and I were at the airport, waiting for a flight that would take us on a week's honeymoon to a couple of islands in Greece, and she said, "Your cousin Alan, I was just thinking. He's a great guy, but he has the saddest eyes."

"Really? I never noticed that. I think he can be very funny—well, not funny-funny but witty."

"Yes, but his eyes struck me as so sad."

I shrugged. She was a very perceptive person, I thought, but sometimes you can take that too far.

After all, what did Alan have to be sad about?

My work, it's important to mention, wasn't going well at this time. My last book wasn't doing what the publisher—or I—had hoped for, and though I'd had one bestseller, nothing can sour a publisher more on your next book than poor sales of your previous one. So I knew I had to come up with a super idea for a new one; but not only didn't I have anything that I thought would please them, I had no ideas that pleased me. I was also having trouble with the national magazines: Ideas I pitched to them kept bouncing back. I'd continued writing for the two true detective magazines out of loyalty to Sam Haggerty; and now the only one I kept selling to was *Detective Eye*—his other magazine had folded—though I was wishing I could finally give it up.

At least once or twice a week I'd get a call from Haggerty, whom I could picture lighting one cigarette with the butt of another as he held the phone to his ear.

"Anything new in the hopper? How about that case…"

And he'd rattle off a crime that he'd read about or heard of on TV. Or I would call him about a murder, either a new one or one that had just been tried in court, and after I'd interviewed the main detectives who'd handled it, it would take me three days at most to write the 5,000-word story. Then it would carry one of my several pen names, under which would be a Sam Haggerty invention:

SPECIAL INVESTIGATOR FOR *Detective Eye*.

Chapter Thirteen

A sign on the highway to South Minton said FOOD LODGING GAS 1 MI at the next turnoff. He didn't plan to take it but when he had about a quarter-mile to go he made a fast decision to do it, then pulled into the parking lot of a hotel, the STEPHAN HOUSE. It was only about three and the snow had stopped again, so there was nothing to stop him from just driving on. But he was only about a hundred miles from the town and he still didn't know what he was going to do.

The lobby was empty, the only person there the clerk behind the counter. He checked in and took the elevator to the fourth floor. The room looked gray when he walked in; *was* gray, until he opened the blinds and the sunlight poured in. He put his attaché case on a chair; it held a change of clothing. Although he hadn't expected to sleep over on his way to South Minton, he had thought he might on the drive home.

He sat down on the side of the bed, then leaned back against a pillow. His mind couldn't stop racing, questioning everything he must have already asked himself a thousand times. Like, let's say he did go through with it, what's the first thing he would do when he got there? He would have to find a copy of the *Breeze* or any other newspaper for July 8, of course—but no, that was wrong: It would have to be the next day's paper, that's the one that would have carried the story if there was a story to carry. Also, he still hadn't decided whether he should go to the *Breeze*'s office for back copies or to the library. In either case, how could he do it without stirring up suspicion, without some giveaway look on his face, perhaps a quiver in his voice or of his hands?

Although he wasn't hungry, he forced himself to go downstairs for some dinner. Afterward he looked around the lobby to see if they had a shop that sold newspapers or paperbacks but though there was one that displayed gift items it was closed. He went over to the desk to see if they at least had some booklets, perhaps describing the area, and was a little surprised to see two or three newspapers on the far side of the counter. They were copies of that morning's local paper, free for guests.

Back in the room, he started to look through the paper but his mind began to drift. Almost without being aware of it, he began thinking of that long-ago little girl, trying again to assure himself that she was alive, that she was a grown woman now, married perhaps and with children. What always amazed him when he thought of her was that there were long periods of time when he *didn't* think of her. Once again he found himself wondering who and what she was, whether Indian or Pakistani or an Arab or a gypsy or maybe a Latino. And who had been with her out on the beach, waiting for her return—parents, guardians, brothers and sisters?

He turned on the TV to the dumbest show he could find, but nothing could quite relax him. He opened the newspaper to the sports section and read about teams and games he had no interest in. Then, as he turned the pages, his eyes settled on one small news story, not so much because of the heading GIRL'S BODY IDENTIFIED IN PARK, but because its dateline read "Philadelphia, PA."

He had made it a practice never to read any story about a murder. Never a complete story, that is; no more than the first paragraph. So though he did know that a girl, an eleven-year-old middle-school student in Philadelphia named Elizabeth Harmann, had been missing for several days, this was the first he knew that her body had been found. She had been raped and strangled.

He threw the paper to the side.

For moments it was as if the police would be coming to question him.

Chapter Fourteen

Alan had been out jogging the afternoon he heard from my mother about his mother.

"Alan," she said, and she began crying. "It's terrible, it's gotten worse. I can't handle it any more. She just threw something at me. It didn't hit me but she threw something. And she's in one of those periods where she doesn't recognize me."

"I'll be right over."

His mother and my mother were living together in a pleasant apartment in the suburbs. His mother had started deteriorating mentally within months after his father's death, and Alan had been paying a woman to help my mother take care of her. But the woman had recently quit.

Not surprisingly, his mother seemed somewhat herself by the time he got there; this happened often. She not only smiled as he kissed her but she said, "Alan," and afterward, "Lawyer."

"How are you, mom?"

"Good." But then she started slipping away again. "It's just night. Nobody."

Kneeling in front of her, he looked over at my mother. She shrugged her shoulders. Then his mother

said, clearly, something she had said to me and surely
to him at his father's funeral:

"It was just like a walk around the block."

Only this time, instead of saying it to him, she seemed
to be saying it to his father.

He looked at her as she was sitting in a living room
chair, a little smile on her lips. He couldn't help think
of the times when he was a kid that she wanted him
to wear rubbers in the rain. And wouldn't let him go
outside when he had all of a ninety-nine degree tem-
perature, which she and his father must have thought
was like a two-hundred degree fever. And the creek
that ran through the woods near our houses, only a foot
or two at its deepest, how it was the curse of her life in
that she was always warning him against falling in and
drowning.

Mom, he thought now, you worried about the
wrong things.

A couple of weeks later, I helped him move his
mother, who had been diagnosed with early-onset
Alzheimer's, into a nursing home. Anna had suggested
that she should come to her place, but though Alan
was tempted he didn't want to put a special burden on
Anna. After tours of several places he'd selected the
one he considered the best. His mother put up no fuss
when he and my mother and I took her there.

Coincidentally, he would learn something exciting
that same day that he would never be able to share
with her. By now he had been approved for the board

of the Foundation, and that evening he got a call at his apartment from Elsa Tomlinson. She didn't ask him any questions; she simply stated a fact.

"I didn't want to call you about this at your office. But I want you here working with me. Right under me, as executive vice president or whatever title I can figure out. I want to groom you to take over, though it'll depend on you how that works out. Now don't say yes, no, maybe. Come in and let's talk."

He saw her the following day, and the upshot was that he was to start in a month.

Chapter Fifteen

When Alan woke at the Stephan House he felt strangely refreshed, as though nothing of importance was on his mind. But then the realization that this was the last leg of his trip sent a quick hot beating through his chest. It was still dark out, and he turned on the lamp on the night table and picked up his wristwatch and glanced at it. It was twenty of six.

It was only when he was walking back from the bathroom and saw the open newspaper over on the chair that he remembered the Elizabeth Harmann murder. He felt the urge to rush over and stuff the paper in the wastebasket; didn't even want it in the room.

Whoever did that to her, whoever committed all of those horrendous rapes and murders he'd tried to avoid knowing about over the years, those people were different from him, weren't they? Weren't they?

By the time he went down to the lobby he had calmed himself considerably. If a murder in Philly could be reported way up here near the Cape, wouldn't an unsolved murder on the Cape have been reported at some time in Philly?

He drove away from the hotel slowly, filled with doubts again but telling himself he was going to do this today, finish what he had started, find out once and for all. But every so often he had to take a deep breath. Then, when he was about twenty miles into Cape Cod on Route 6, he almost froze in panic. A police car was parked angled on this side of the road, its lights glittering.

A short line of cars had slowed ahead of him. He could see an officer standing next to a car, apparently talking to the driver. Occasionally, as the line moved forward, the officer would lean toward a window, then motion ahead with his arm. But it was only when Alan got much closer that he could see that he was directing traffic around a two-car accident.

About an hour later Alan was driving between a thick line of trees on either side of the road that told him across the years that he either was approaching a turnoff to South Minton or had possibly already passed it. All he knew for sure was that the ocean was to his right; other than that, his mind had gone blank. Then he saw a sign by an intersection, perhaps the same one that was there that day fifteen years ago: SOUTH MINTON.

The lane his father had turned into had to be one of these several lanes he was now beginning to pass. And then, about a mile or so away, would be that other lane where…

He turned into one of them at random, thinking as he did of the old saying about a criminal returning to the scene of his crime. All he knew was that he wanted to go back through the years, to look, to see.

The trees were skeletal in the cold, the ground hard and uneven, some of the limbs layered with snow. He came to the top of the dune, as if to an old nightmare, and stopped with a heavy foot on the brake. The ocean lay ahead, bright blue, with just a slight curve of waves at the fringe. He kept the motor running, the heater of course on. He couldn't believe he had pulled in here and was actually remaining even though he was aware that someone might have seen him turn in. And that a face might suddenly appear at his window.

What are you doing here, sir, and who are you?

Still, he couldn't make himself turn around or back out. Not yet, not yet.

Which lane was this, if either of the two? He couldn't tell for sure, but soon he began thinking of it as the one where they'd parked the motor home, the seats facing the dune, though at a slight angle. His father was still behind the wheel, his mother in her usual seat next to him, and he in one of the seats behind them, though sometimes he'd sit next to his father, hungering with a teenager's hunger to be able to take that wheel.

He thought of the coziness of that motor home, of his bunk along the side and their little room in back with its accordion-like doorway. And how they would all watch TV at night, or read under the lamps or play gin rummy.

Soon he saw two people, a man and a woman, materialize in the distance on the beach. They wore heavy coats and woolen caps down over their ears in the cold and wind. He hadn't seen a single person that time they'd been here, and for a few moments he just sat watching them walking closer. And then he came out of it and back into the icy reality that no one must see him. He backed away from the dune fast, then made a U-turn and headed toward the road, the car bumping over the hard ruts. When he came to the road he stopped just long enough to make sure no cars were in sight in either direction. Then he drove to the inter-section that led to South Minton.

He remembered how he had pleaded with his father not to go there, and then how he'd sprawled across the sofa not wanting to be seen through the windows. He hadn't seen a second's worth of the town. Now he saw that the turn-off led, after a couple of miles of cottages and woods, to a frozen-looking bay fronted by shops, houses and eateries, quite a few of the places art shops and many with the look of being closed for the winter. He drove through a tangle of streets, some with much larger houses, past a firehouse, then—almost startling him—a small police station, and now what announced itself to be the Municipal Building. He was looking for whatever building might house the *Breeze* but he couldn't find it. However, he did find the library, a long low building that still had several strings of Christmas lights dangling, darkened, from the roof.

He parked at the curb across the street and looked over at it. The enormity of what he hoped to do was becoming overwhelming. How could he, a stranger, go in there and ask for God-knows-how-many old issues without stirring suspicion, without someone asking what're you looking for, can I help? What would he answer? He'd assumed he could get away with some kind of generality, but that was stupid, stupid.

Though it seemed as if he'd been thinking about this forever, he had to think it out more, he just couldn't—

He pulled away from the curb. He drove slowly, telling himself this was just to give him time to think; but when he came to the street that led back to Route 6, he took it—and drove faster. And once out on the road he almost floored the pedal.

He could never go into that building. Never!

But then, about ten miles away, he pulled into an abandoned service station and parked, the motor running.

He had to think harder. As if he hadn't all these years! As if he hadn't gone back and forth in his head a million times—do this, don't do that, you must find out, but why?—you must, but you didn't *kill* her, yet you've got to know!

He tried to focus on what had finally come together to bring him here.

One was another call, about month ago, from Elsa Tomlinson. "Alan, I hate to rush you, but can you start next week? The week after at the latest? It's very important, I need you here."

He hadn't even told his firm yet he would be leaving.

The second was a message on his answering

machine. From Anna. It was a simple one:

"I'm going to sleep, honey, but I just want to say I miss you."

He stood there, staring at the machine. There was nothing special about the message, but it made him feel hollowed out. They'd never said they loved each other, but he never wanted to more than right now.

But he couldn't—not until he learned the truth.

Chapter Sixteen

The firm he was with was a large one though far from the largest—thirty-two lawyers. He said good morning to his secretary at her desk in front of his office: He shared her with an associate in the adjoining office. His office overlooked much of downtown and the Delaware River, ten stories below, which reflected his fast-rising status in the firm. He looked at a few just-delivered letters on his desk, then put them down without opening them. He took a deep breath and walked to the managing partner's office.

"I just want to let you know," he told him, "that I'm going to be leaving the firm."

"Oh?" Just that, with almost no change of expression. "I'm sorry to hear that. Is it rude of me to ask where you'll be going?"

"Not at all." He told him about the Foundation.

"Well, you were on the move here and we'll miss you. What can I say but good luck?"

"Thanks. Look, I won't be leaving for two weeks if necessary, so—"

The man smiled. "Try for tomorrow. Or even today if you can clear things up."

*

That night, sitting with Anna on her sofa, Alan told her about his resigning and moving on. She hugged him tight and said how happy she was for him, but afterward there was something obviously sad about her. She was frowning, seemed to be deep within herself.

"Anna, what's wrong?"

She looked startled, began to shake her head and then stopped. It was a few moments before she looked at him.

"Why did you really call me that time?"

"What time?"

"The first time. Why did you call me?"

"Because I wanted to. I had the feeling you were someone special. Why did you agree to go out with me?"

She didn't answer. Then she said, "What do you think of me now?"

"I think you're wonderful."

"Not just easy?"

"Oh Christ, Anna, you've got to be kidding."

She seemed close to tears. "I'm sorry. But there are so many creeps. I think I met most of them the first year I was here. They think because you're a nurse and you're young…"

He put his arms around her.

"You think you won't fall for it, you think you're too smart, but then you do. You think they love you. And then it turns out you had no idea at all what was going on in their heads. It was all a lie."

Her body was rigid at first, but then softened a little

and she let herself come against him, her head on his shoulder. He wanted to say things to her, things that would help, but somehow he knew that words would never do it, that just holding her was the better way, the only way.

"Alan?"

"Yes, Anna."

But she just shook her head against him, without looking up, and then seemed to creep into him even more. He rubbed her back, her shoulders, put his cheek on her hair.

She said, "Thank you." It was muffled against his chest.

He wanted to say how can you thank me, I should be thanking you. But he didn't. Instead he brushed at the hair that had fallen over her forehead. She raised her head and he kissed her lips, softly. Her lips opened and for moments they just breathed into each other, just breathed. And now he was unbuttoning her blouse and she made a few quick attempts at trying to help him. They didn't even go to the bedroom. Not then anyway, later yes, but not then in their haste. And now they were part of each other, joined and yet trying to get even closer, and then collapsing, finally lying in each other's arms so still except for the beating of their hearts.

And it was then, lying against her, that he knew— *really* knew—he couldn't put off learning the truth.

Chapter Seventeen

Easing his car onto Route 6 again, he began heading slowly back to South Minton. He still wasn't sure he would do it, could make himself do it. Nor did he know as he drove on the turnoff to the town; he was even glad for a delay when he realized he was confused about where the library was. He began taking different streets at random, found himself at the bay again, saw a few people walking against the wind, kept making turns; and then he saw the building looming just ahead.

He pulled up along the curb, behind two or three other cars. He sat there looking at the library building. Though the heater was on, he felt a chill go through him and he took hold of his hands to keep them from trembling. He rubbed them warm, then almost on impulse turned off the motor, pushed open the door and walked quickly to the front steps.

Two people were behind the front desk, a woman who turned out to be the librarian, and a young man in his twenties who was lifting books out of a cart. A woman was sitting at one of the tables toward the back of the library while another woman was looking at the stacks.

The librarian, a woman who looked to be in her fifties, smiled as he came up to the desk.

"Hello there. Can I help you?"

Afraid that his voice would shake, he said, "I hope so. Do you carry old back copies of the *Breeze*?"

"Yes we do. What issue are you looking for?"

"Problem is I'm not sure. It would be somewhere from May '89 to November '91."

"Oh my, that is old. Let me see. I want to make sure of something."

He watched tensely as she went to a computer. When she came back she said, "I wanted to double-check how far it goes back online. And so far it's only to '92. But we should have all the earlier issues stored downstairs. Sam here will start bringing them up if you'd like."

Alan sat down at a long table, and after a while Sam began bringing them up on a cart, fifteen issues at a time for him to go through before Sam brought up others. Wanting only to get to July 8th, he had to pretend to be going through each earlier one carefully. But fortunately the papers were thin in May, growing thicker as summer approached, and now July—

His body was icy as he lifted the July 8th issue off the pile and put it down in front of him. And it was with a burst of joy that he saw nothing about any crime on the first page, and nothing on the pages after that. But then he remembered that the earliest the story could have appeared would have been the following morning.

He reached for that paper. And within seconds his heart felt as if it had exploded.

The headline, in huge screaming print, read:

GIRL FOUND MURDERED
IN WOODS BY BEACH

He saw a large picture of her face, the face he'd lived with for so long, narrow and pretty and wide-eyed, posed in a formal portrait at a slight angle and with a shy smile. Not just a pretty but a beautiful face, with a name under it, Susheela Kapasi, and her age, thirteen—she had looked even younger! Next to her picture was a view of the scene, with the trees he remembered and even the kite. And the story—he could hardly read it. He caught only fragments, isolated words: "strangled," "brutal." Phrases. Something about her father finding the body.

He wanted to read all of it, not only the whole story but the stories from the next day and the days after, but he looked up and saw the librarian staring at him. He didn't know what caused what happened next, but he'd probably brushed against the pile of papers in his panic. A wave of copies crashed to the floor; he bent over quickly and began gathering them up. Then when he sat up he saw that the librarian was gone and that Sam was by himself, watching him from the counter. Alan could only think that she might be calling the police—a suspicious stranger!— and he knew that he had to gather up all the papers and not walk out fast or break into the run he was fighting against. He brought the papers to the desk and even looked at Sam to thank him, but Sam was looking down at something on the counter—deliberately, Alan thought. He walked out, and then hurried with long strides down the steps and along the sidewalk to his car.

He pulled away fast—but then for the next five or ten minutes didn't know which street to take to get to Route 6 and away from South Minton. He tried several, twice finding himself at places he'd already been to. Then he heard the whine of a siren. He had no idea where it was coming from or where it was heading to or if it had anything to do with him. He pulled to the curb and looked to the side, hoping that the wail, if it was on this street, would just go by him. And then it died away, going on to somewhere else.

But going on to where? The library?

He drove on, taking two or three wrong turns in his confusion, searching for some kind of landmark and hoping that he wasn't just heading back to the library. He saw a service station—God, he needed gas but mustn't stop!—and he was sure he'd seen it before. There were two streets leading away from it. He picked one—and in front of him, soon, was Route 6. He turned onto it, nearly skidding.

He forced himself to slow down, to drive just a little above the speed limit, though several cars sped by him. He felt his heart racing. And through his fear ran the thought that he *couldn't* have…strangled her, that his arm hadn't been that tight around her throat, that his other hand had just taken hold of her shoulder and halter strap…

But gradually, as if through a mist that years of hoping and praying and denial had formed, he was back among those trees again. And this time…this time his arm was cinched tight and then tighter around that fragile throat.

Chapter Eighteen

Kill yourself or give yourself up.

One or the other.

No other alternative.

And yet his eyes kept frantically checking the gas, seeing the needle almost on empty but afraid to stop because he had to get away, must get away. When he finally did see a service station he started to drive past it, but then stopped and backed up and turned in at the pump the farthest back from the street.

Kill yourself or give yourself up!

Yet as the tank was slowly filling he was suddenly frantic with the thought that the librarian may have gone outside and gotten his license number, that he could be stopped at any point or might drive home only to find police cars waiting for him.

Driving away, once again he tried to be careful not to go too fast or too slow, though at times his body felt as if it were running ahead of the car.

Why did I ever go up there? It struck him that he could have checked a lot more newspapers on his computer, but it had been as though he wanted to come here, just as he had wanted to see that lane again. He had known how dangerous it was, hadn't he? But why, why *now* when his life had become so good?

He loved Anna, she loved him. And his work at the Foundation these first two weeks was so promising. Why had he ruined everything?

Even at the library, why had he gotten so scared and hurried out? So he'd dropped the newspapers, and the librarian had disappeared from where she'd been; so what? What he'd done was make a suspicious ass out of himself!

But look, he tried assuring himself, he could be wrong about the whole thing. They still might not be suspicious of him. Maybe it was all in his head.

Yes, but what about that siren he'd heard?

And what about—the thing he could no longer deceive himself about—his having murdered that girl? Though for the moment he was consumed only with the need to flee, his brain, his whole body felt in flames as though the crime and its savagery were all brand new.

Driving on, he was trying to convince himself of the wisdom of giving up. After all, he'd only been a kid when it happened and he hadn't meant it—meant to kill her, that is; he'd panicked—and he'd never done anything wrong before or after. He'd been a good kid and he was a good guy, he'd done well in school, he was a lawyer, he was vice president and on the board of directors of this great charitable foundation. And though he would have to face a firestorm of publicity, of cameras in his face and on his handcuffed hands in back, of being dissected forever on CNN and Fox News and by Larry King and a hundred others, he'd get through it, he'd live through the shame and—

But then, as he'd done many times before, he thought of all the stories he'd read or heard about, of people arrested years after their crime, like that fellow in Connecticut, some sort of Kennedy family relative, sentenced to twenty years to life for the murder of a girl years ago.

Twenty to *life!*

It scared him almost to paralysis. How could he live with this absolute terror of police he felt spiraling through him as he drove up to his apartment house, the same terror he'd felt fifteen years ago returning home from that trip? But, as then, no cops were waiting to converge on him. A couple of people standing by the elevators smiled and he thought he smiled back. Everything seemed so normal. Then when he got to his apartment he saw the morning's paper lying folded in front of the door. And the part of the headline he could see read:

SLAIN GIRL...

He grabbed it up, as though somehow he had already become encircled.

But it had nothing to do with him. The police, he saw quickly, had arrested the killer of the girl whose raped body had been found in the park.

Almost the first thing he did in the apartment, despite begging himself not to at least for a while, was go to the computer and type in the name Susheela Kapasi. A page of links appeared, with references to others he could open when he finished these. He tried three or four of them, what seemed to be the earliest ones. Susheela was described as an excellent student, a high school freshman who had had some childhood disease that affected her physical growth. She was the daughter of Indian immigrants, her father a professor at MIT, her mother an artist. She'd been an only child, a "beautiful, special girl," as her father described her, who had been picnicking with them on the beach and then left them to run after her downed kite; a girl who'd wanted to grow up to be a scientist like him.

Sprinkled through the stories were "vicious," "savage," "a community in terror."

Him. It was hard to realize at first, and then not so hard, that they were referring to him.

In addition to the *Breeze*, one of the papers was from a nearby town while another was from Boston and carried a story by the Associated Press. He skipped several years ahead. Her friends had formed a club in her memory early on, and one story was about how they still met and the charity work they performed. Then there was a story two or three years later that retold Susheela's "unsolved murder" and mentioned that both of her parents were dead, her mother from a heart attack and her father, a year after that, in an automobile accident.

He turned off the computer.

His feeling was one of fresh horror that if it weren't for him none of this would ever have happened. But then came another feeling, which he was almost ashamed to admit to himself. Now he would never have to face them.

Meanwhile, the red light on his answering machine was blinking but he didn't care who had called him. He was totally out of that world of friendships and telemarketers. But his throat was parched and he still needed water to drink; his face and hands were sweaty and they had to be washed. And after he drank and washed and dried himself he did go over to the machine. There had been three calls, one from me.

"Hi. It's Colin. I just heard about your appointment. Congratulations. I can't wait to talk to you about it. Call me when you can, will you?"

The second was from an old friend, Gregg Osterly.

"I'm letting you know that Sandy and I are having some people over for dinner this Saturday. Come with a date, come alone, but come. Let me hear from you, buddy."

The third message was from Anna, whom he had promised to call when he got back.

"Just me, honey. I hope you had a successful trip. I just want you to know I won't be home until about eight. Talk to you later."

Standing there he couldn't even remember the lie he had told her about his "trip," only that it had something to do with work, and that he'd be going to Virginia, not the Cape. He had told a different lie to Elsa Tomlinson, one that had something to do with his family, because he'd had to go up there during the week, which meant, of course, that he'd had to take off from work. The library, he had learned through a call, closed at noon on Saturdays and he had been afraid he might need more time.

He suddenly became aware that he was being pounded by music that was coming through the walls from next door.

He'd heard it the moment he walked into the apartment but it hadn't bothered him the way it did now. An architect and his wife lived there, two nice polite people when they weren't drunk. He must have called them about their stereo at least four times in the past three months, and each time they were friendly and lowered it. Now he told himself to let it alone, he had enough on his mind, just let it alone. And as it turned out, he was right. This time his neighbor was angry when he answered the phone.

His first words were a drunken, "Yeah? Yeah?"

"Joe, this is Alan next door. Will you—"

"Yeah, Alan-next-door, what d'you want?"

"Would you please lower the music for me? Please?"

"Lower the music?" he shouted. "Lower it? That's all I hear from you! Don't you like classical music? Don't you like good music?"

"I like good music but you're playing it too loud. Lower it, will you?"

"Go to sleep! Go outside! Take a walk! Don't bother me any more!"

"I'm just asking you to lower it a little!"

"Don't yell at me! Who the hell are you to yell at

me! Goddamn you, you call me again I'm calling the police! You hear me? You hear me?"

And with that he hung up. Alan sat there, gripping the phone. He didn't know what he was afraid of most at that moment—the police? Or the rage in him, the feeling that given a chance he would kill the son of a bitch.

Chapter Nineteen

He didn't know if he would ever call Anna again. Though he'd thought it before, this was different. He felt apart from everyone and everything, felt no longer even a small part of the world he had always known. But then at about eight she called from a cell phone in her car.

"Honey," she said brightly, "I'm so glad you're home. I'm just leaving work and I thought you might have tried me at home."

"No, I just got in."

"Tell me, how did it go?"

"Okay. All right."

A pause. "Honey, is something wrong? You don't sound right."

"No, no," he answered quickly, "everything's all right."

"I was wondering if you've had dinner. I know it's late."

"No, but I'm not hungry."

"Oh, you've got to have something. You should, you really should. What about this? I didn't eat either. Can I bring us something?"

And all at once, hearing her voice in what was now

the silence of his apartment—the music had stopped—
he didn't want to be alone.

She was there in about forty minutes, carrying a
large bag of Chinese food. He tried not to just pick at
his food and later even managed a joke about their for-
tune cookie messages. Then, while they were carrying
the dishes to the sink, he heard her say, in anguish,
"Terrible. Dreadful. Terrible."

He looked at her sharply, and then in the direction
she was looking. And there on top of the trashcan in
the kitchen was that morning's newspaper, with the
headline: SLAIN GIRL CONFESSION.

He had just glanced at it enough to know that a
46-year-old drifter, a paroled child molester, had
admitted to her rape-murder. And now even as Alan
wanted to cry out his old cry of I'm different, she was
saying:

"You know, I don't believe in capital punishment, I
really don't. But when I see something like this...I
don't care what they do to him. Right now I wish they
would tear him apart."

A big part of him wanted Anna to go home, to be by
himself, maybe to be able to spend more time at the
computer. But when they got in bed he put his arms
around her and lay with his cheek against hers, so glad
she was there. Her hands grew tight on his shoulders.

"I feel your heart," she said.

He nodded.

"Do you feel mine?" she asked.

"Yes. Yes, I feel your heart."

She lifted her face and kissed his forehead, his cheeks.

"Honey"—she brushed at his hair, looking at him—"you seem so sad. Are you unhappy with me?"

"Oh no, don't ever say that."

"But you do, you look sad."

"I'm not sad at all," and he shook his head and even smiled. He put his hand on her chin and lifted her face and kissed her. She opened her lips and they drew in each other's tongue.

"Oh honey," she said, "I love you."

He wanted to say, "I love you, too," but he felt more than ever that he had no right to say it, to wrap her even tighter into his life. But he was also aware that he was thinking: *Oh God, I can never give myself up!*

He felt someone grabbing him in the night, and he half sprang up in bed only to realize through the booming of his heart that it was Anna.

"Darling, darling," she was saying.

He lay back slowly, scared only that he had screamed something—a name? a confession? But she was saying, "It's okay, darling, it's okay, you just had a bad dream." And now as they were both lying back, arms around each other, she was saying, "What was it? Can you tell me?"

He shook his head. "I don't know." And he didn't. Only that he'd been running across some kind of field.

He imagined it had been from police, though he couldn't remember.

"That's awful," she was saying. "I know what it's like, though I haven't had a nightmare like that in years."

Soon she fell asleep again but he lay awake for at least an hour more. The next he heard was the sound of the shower in the morning, and then she came out of the bathroom, a towel wrapped around her.

She said, "Don't get up. It's too early for you, you don't have to go in until later. I'll have coffee at the place."

"No, I'm getting up."

They had coffee together, sitting at the kitchen table. He didn't want to go into the hall for the newspaper, didn't want to know about anything right now that was going on in the world. Nor did he want her to leave. He dreaded being alone even for the hour or so before he would go off to the office. And how he dreaded walking in there.

They kissed before he opened the door for her, and then he walked with her down the hall and waited until she got on the elevator. He picked up the newspaper by his door and, after glancing at the front page to see if there was anything about the Harmann murder, he put it on a table and went to finish dressing. The apartment was so silent that the silence seemed a noise of its own. His computer was on a desk in the living room, and the temptation was to pull up the *Breeze*'s Web site to see if there was anything on it about a suspicious incident at the library. But he didn't want to know if there was. He wanted to go in to the Foundation thinking that he had probably imagined the whole thing, that he had panicked for no reason.

He picked up the newspaper again to see if there was anything about the Harmann girl's murder on one of the inside pages. Nothing on the second page. But on the third page was a picture of the killer, a man named Harold Luder. Again Alan just read the story in bits and pieces. It said little new about the man, other than that he had been paroled two years ago after serving twelve years for molesting a ten-year-old girl.

Alan stuffed the whole paper into the trashcan.

Again he was thinking this isn't me. How many times over the years he had tested himself by looking at little girls, mostly those in ads, and there'd never been that sort of a desire, that sort of a feeling.

The offices of the Foundation took up an entire floor of a fourteen story building in downtown Philadelphia. His office was next to Elsa Tomlinson's. It was a spacious office, with a look of high corporate position. On his desk, waiting for him, was a small neat pile of proposals for grants from inner city ballet companies along the East Coast. He'd already seen them, and they had been returned to him with comments from the staff. There would be a meeting on it later in the day.

Mid-morning there was a coffee break: A vendor brought in a cart of coffee, tea, sodas and cakes, and people streamed to it from their offices and desks.

One of the things he'd cautioned himself about as he'd walked into the building was not to look sad, not to show the face that Anna had seen.

Elsa, he couldn't help noticing, barely acknowledged him as they stood around the cart. Although she hadn't said anything, his taking a couple of days off for a personal matter so soon after joining obviously bothered her.

Ron Jameson, one of the division vice presidents, a man who always wore a bowtie, asked, "How did your trip go?"

"Okay. Good. I'm glad it's over."

"How," he came back softly, glancing toward Elsa standing far from the cart now, "was it taken?"

Alan pretended he didn't know what he meant. But he did have the feeling that Jameson, a man in his fifties, was one of those who resented him.

"It was fine," he said, and he managed to drift away. But it was only to join a small group that was talking about the Elizabeth Harmann murder.

"Her poor family…"

He went back in his office.

This time when he came home, into the quiet of his apartment, he went straight to the computer and logged into the *Breeze's* Web site. There was nothing in it about the library. He told himself to quit now, to shut down the machine. But instead he did a search for Susheela Kapasi's name again, went to links he hadn't opened yet. One of these was under the name Mack McKinney. And this name had several links of its own.

The first one he opened revealed a picture as well as a story.

The picture was of a man Alan had seen on television several times over the years—seen, that is, for a few moments in passing as he flipped through the channels. He'd been on programs such as Larry King, *America's Most Wanted*, some Court TV shows. But Alan had never stopped to listen to him for more than a minute or two.

Now he read that Mack McKinney was a 67-year-old retired New Jersey state police detective whose twelve-year-old daughter had been raped and murdered eighteen years ago by a handyman who was now serving a life sentence. Sometime after the murder, McKinney had started a foundation in her name to help publicize and finance investigations into old unsolved murders of children. One of the cases he was actively involved in was that of Susheela Kapasi.

"It's work I want do until the day I die," he was quoted as saying.

And his eyes, Alan felt, were staring at him.

Chapter Twenty

His friend Gregg Osterly, who had left a message on his answering machine inviting him to dinner, was someone he had known since college; they frequently played squash together in the gym Alan went to once or twice a week. A Ford dealer, he lived with his wife, two children and widowed father-in-law on a ten-acre farm about twenty miles outside the city. Alan had no intention of going—it was an effort just to go to work and be with people there—but when he neglected calling him back, Gregg phoned him again on Friday evening when Anna was with him.

"Hey buddy," he said, "did you get my message?"

"Yes, I'm sorry I didn't get back to you, I was out of town."

"Well, you're in town now. So tell me you're coming. I don't like seeing my wife cry."

"Hold on." Why couldn't he just say no? But Anna was looking at him, almost as if she had heard the conversation, and with his hand over the receiver he told her about the invitation.

"I'd love to go if you want to," she said.

The invitation was for six o'clock on Saturday but he picked Anna up about ten in the morning and they headed out to Amish country, about thirty miles away, driving up a one-lane road, Route 340, that cut mostly through farmland and villages with names such as Blue Ball, Intercourse, and Bird in Hand. As they drove, and even though they'd both seen it before, they admired, as if it were a different planet, the Amish in their horse-clopping buggies, the horse-and-mule-plowed fields, the houses with long clotheslines of black garments, and, since many of the homes had no electricity even though electric lines ran from pole to pole along the road, the windmills that stood on their grounds. They stopped at antique shops, bought nothing though he kept asking her to, had a good lobster tail lunch without worrying what they would have for dinner, and even took a few-mile train ride through the fields.

There were two other couples at Gregg's, both of whom Alan knew. Gregg took an immediate liking to Anna, had her sit next to him at the table, and afterward took her on a tour of the large farmhouse. Alan walked with them as he led her from room to room, pointing out antiques and what, in the restoring of the place, was new and what was originally there. His children, twin six-year-old girls, were playing in their bedroom while his father-in-law was in an upstairs study, watching television.

"Dad, you know Alan, of course. I want you to meet Anna."

His father-in-law stood up, held out his hand to them.

"Can you imagine," Gregg was saying, "Dad here

didn't want to eat with us?" But Alan barely heard his words. He was staring, frozen, at the screen.

The Larry King program was on. And the retired state policeman, Mack McKinney, was one of three men sitting across from him.

"Oh you know I ate earlier," Gregg's father-in-law was saying.

"Yeah, I know, I know. I know you."

Alan only wished they would shut up; he couldn't hear, he was straining to hear words.

"Well, let's move along," Gregg said.

"I want to watch this for a second," Alan said.

"Well, I'm going to show Anna the barn. We'll be out there."

But in only the few seconds it took for Alan to turn from them back to the screen, commercials were on. He stood there waiting, anxiously. Had they been talking about the murder? Maybe about what had happened at the library? He wanted to ask Gregg's father-in-law but was afraid that even a little show of curiosity would point to his guilt.

Now Larry King and the three men were back on.

Instead of talking about any particular crime, Larry said, "I want to introduce former detective Mack McKinney once again, a man who's long been involved in helping solve or draw attention to unsolved crimes. And fortunately for us all, he has been mighty successful at it."

Alan stared on, wondering what might be coming next.

"I know," Larry said to McKinney, "you've gone into this many times. But I would like you to do it again for those listeners who might not know of the tragedy in your life that brought you to this tremendous work. You had a daughter Sharon, who was murdered at the age of twelve back in 1986. Would you tell us something about that?"

"Yes," McKinney said, clearing his throat. "My wife and I came home after doing some shopping and we found that she wasn't there. This was only about six o'clock and it didn't really alarm us. But after about an hour we began calling her friends and one of them told us that Sharon had been at her house but had left to go home at around five. The houses were relatively close, so she would have walked. That's the last she was seen alive.

"It wasn't until two weeks later that her body was found in the woods about a mile from our home. Searchers had gone over the woods repeatedly, but this time a neighbor noticed a small mound of dirt under some leaves. And under that..."

He stopped. His eyes were glazed with tears.

"She'd been tortured and raped."

"And her killer," Larry said, "was a handyman you knew. Someone who had done some work around your house."

"That's right."

"And who received life without parole."

"Yes. I've been asked so often if that's closure for us.

It isn't. But I don't know if the death penalty would be either. Nothing really is."

Alan slipped out of the room, his pulse beating in his temples. It was a moment or two before he became aware of how much he hated, how much he *loathed*, whoever had killed that child.

After dropping Anna off at her apartment he headed back to his place about one in the morning. He had a reason for not staying over. Worried about the first half of the program he had missed, he was anxious to see if it might be repeated, as programs often were late at night.

In his apartment, he went straight to the trash can for the TV pages of that day's paper, found them and looked to see if the program might be running again at any early morning hour. No, it wouldn't. But he read the brief description of the program he'd seen and released a long breath. It had been about a murder he knew nothing about.

This feeling of reprieve was only to last until morning, when he saw Mack McKinney's face in the paper again. It was as if the man were following him, watching him, drawing closer.

Chapter Twenty-One

The picture was about the size of a postage stamp yet it loomed in front of him like a billboard.

He generally didn't look through the TV supplement of the Sunday paper unless there was something in particular he wanted to check on. And there wasn't that morning. He just happened to be gathering up the thick paper before leaving to visit his mother when several pages of the section fell open and, while straightening them, he saw McKinney's face.

He was to be on a cable show called *The Justice Road* next Tuesday at 9 PM.

This hunter, the item read, *of child murderers and predators…*

It said nothing about what he would be discussing. But as Alan stared at that face, it was as if the man were already talking—to him.

Driving to the nursing home he thought of something that brought a kind of comfort, if anything horrendous can be called comfort; and it was that his mother was out of it, would never know the truth about him even if someone shouted it into her face.

But she wasn't out of it that day. That was the weird part. At least she wasn't out of it for a few minutes.

She had aged terribly in just a few years. She still

had a broad face but it was sunken between the bones. And her hair was almost white. She looked at him from her wheelchair with clear blue eyes as he approached her in the lounge, then, recognizing him, she said with a smile, "Alan." And then nodded when he asked how she was.

He'd brought her two new nightgowns, and a nurse took one of them from the box and held it up for her.

"Isn't this lovely what your son brought you?"

His mother looked at it with that same smile, and then at the other nightgown, which the nurse also held up. Then she looked at him.

"You were always a good boy."

"Oh, Mom." He was holding her hand.

A minute or two passed, during which her look gradually became a stare that was now focused on her lap.

He said, "Mom?" But she didn't look at him or, a little later, seem to notice when he kissed her goodbye.

As he walked away, he thought of what she'd said about his always having been "good boy." And how her being alert for a time had scared him.

That evening he took Anna to dinner, and afterward they came back to his place. They were there no more than ten minutes when the phone rang. A young voice, a girl's, immediately said, "Hi lover. I really want you."

He could also hear another girl's voice, though unintelligible, in the background.

He started to hang up but then glanced quickly at

the little panel on his phone. It listed an area code and phone number.

"I would love to fuck you," the first girl said. "Would you like to fuck me? And I'm good at sucking too. Do you have a large dick?"

He covered the mouthpiece of the receiver. The area code was the same as Anna's parents', but not the number.

He didn't know what to say, whether to tell her.

"Honey"—Anna stood up from the sofa and came over—"is something wrong?"

"Look, do you recognize this area code?"

She looked, then said, puzzled, "Yes. But I don't know the number. Who is it?"

He heard a click as the girls on the other end hung up. He set the receiver down. Anna's eyes widened as he told her the kind of call it was. Her hand flew to her mouth.

"Oh God. My sister, oh that bitch!"

"I don't think it was your sister. She didn't talk to me when I was up there but I remember her talking to your mother. And I don't think this was her voice."

"Oh, it was her and her friend. She put her friend up to it. I know that bitch, I know that stupid bitch."

"Why would she do it?" But it was such a foolish question he instantly regretted asking it. He could picture that orange-haired girl he'd met, pregnant, playing kids' stupid games.

"Did she ever do this before?"

"Yes!"

"Did you ever tell your parents?"

"Yes!"

"What did they do?"

"Nothing. I don't know. Nothing. She doesn't listen anyway."

She began to cry.

"Look, don't," he said.

"She's such a bitch. And she's a liar, she makes up stories. She tries to spoil everything for me."

He led her back to the sofa and put his arm around her. After a few moments she leaned forward, her forehead against the fingers of one hand.

"I don't deserve you," she said against her hand.

"Oh, stop it. Because your sister's a nut? A kid?"

"I've tried hard to break away from there. How I've tried."

"Honey." He brought her close. "Honey, you have. Now let's forget this, can we? I know I have."

She pressed her cheek against his shoulder.

"I'm scared," she said.

He didn't want to say it but he did. "Of what?"

"That I'm going to lose you. I don't want to lose you. I love you so much."

"Oh, I love you too." It was the first time he'd ever said it to her.

"You didn't have to say that." She didn't look up.

"Then I'll take it back."

"No. No." She looked at him quickly, then put her forefinger to his lips. "Don't. Let it stay said."

❧

Tuesday night he turned on the channel at least ten minutes before the program was to go on. When it did, he saw that Mack McKinney was not the only guest. It was a new show, only a month or so old, and was hosted by a former prosecutor, an attractive youngish-looking woman named Tess Antoni. Her first two guests were a defense attorney and a retired D.A., and they differed strongly about the pardoning of sex offenders. Alan barely listened; he was too intent on what McKinney would be there to talk about.

When McKinney came on Alan was a little surprised by his reaction to how the retired officer looked. He had seen him as a terribly stern man, even when his eyes had teared up when he spoke about his daughter. Now, his was rather a gentle face, his voice soft, his eyes sad.

And somehow, amazingly, though Alan felt startled to his bones, he even saw him that way when, for the first time, he heard him speak the name Susheela Kapasi.

"She was a beautiful girl. Beautiful. I've looked at her picture so many times."

"I understand," Antoni asked, "you weren't there at the beginning of the investigation, is that right?"

"Yes, that's right. I'm from New Jersey and when I retired from the force my wife and I moved to Cape Cod, right near South Minton. That was about two years after her body was found. I've never been officially involved in the investigation but it's one of the cases—and I do hate to call these tragedies 'cases'—it's one of the cases our foundation and I strongly support."

"What about the motive for the murder? There has been some speculation about this, I understand."

"Well, not really. It's believed the intent was sexual assault, but that the killer ran away when her father came looking for her and calling her name."

"It's fifteen years now. Have the police made any progress toward solving it?"

"Let's put it this way. It's still an active case. And now and then leads do come in and every one of them is followed. For instance…"

And then he told of a "stranger"—tall, white, dark hair, perhaps between thirty-two and thirty-five—who had showed up recently in the South Minton public library.

"He asked to see old newspapers. He seemed quite nervous and even dropped some, and after he left, the librarian saw that the latest papers he asked for carried the first stories of the murder. So she very alertly called the police…"

McKinney was going on but for a few moments Alan was still caught up in what he'd just said, that it was only after he returned the papers, not before, that she'd called the police.

"Now this fellow might have absolutely nothing to do with it," McKinney was saying, "but he would be doing the investigation a big favor if he contacted the police and cleared his name."

McKinney then gave a telephone number, which was printed out on the screen.

And then, following this, and as large as the screen itself, was a composite sketch of Alan's face.

Chapter Twenty-Two

He stared at it in shock, then tried telling himself it didn't look like him, not at all, that this was too long and that too wide. Then he went to a mirror and stared at himself, turning his face in different ways, telling himself the nose in the picture was all wrong, he didn't have that kind of chin, that wasn't the way he combed his hair; and yet he didn't know, he didn't know. And the age wasn't exact; he jumped on the fact that he was thirty, not thirty-two to thirty-five, trying to look on it as all the difference in the world.

He went back to his computer. That morning he had checked with the *Breeze* and had seen nothing about the crime. Now he went back to scour it again. But still nothing. The following morning, though, was different.

First, there was a two-column headline: LIBRARY VISITOR SOUGHT IN KAPASI MURDER. And then, underneath, was the sketch.

He read on through wavering vision.

It repeated what McKinney had said about the librarian noticing his "unusual behavior" and "nervousness" and then seeing that the last newspapers he'd been given were from a few days after the murder. The police hadn't revealed at the time that they were interested in speaking to the "stranger," in the hope that he would return. The story emphasized that he still might have a perfectly good explanation for wanting to see the papers.

Alan printed out the sketch and went with it to the mirror, hoping to confirm close up that it didn't really look like him. He kept looking back and forth from the mirror to the picture, from the picture to the mirror, and it did seem to him, with drumming heart, that there was really no similarity. Still, he began playing with the idea of going up to South Minton and saying yes I was here, here I am, I was looking through those papers for this, that. How could they prove otherwise? After all, no one had seen him with her, no one knew that their motor home had been parked a half-mile or so away: That part of the beach had been empty. But he knew almost instantly that he would fall apart under the first questioning, blurt it all out in tears.

And then something else struck him with full force.

The Philly papers! Would they carry the sketch? Would his friends, relatives—*Anna!*—see it? And even though he thought it didn't look like him, was he wrong? Would they know?

He still hadn't picked up his morning paper from outside the door. He went for it, close to panic, placed its various sections on the kitchen table and began going through them.

No.

No, but for how long?

Get 2 Books Every Month...
For the Price of ONE!

☐ **YES! Sign me up for the Hard Case Crime Book Club!**

As long as I choose to stay in the club, I will receive TWO Hard Case Crime books each month — that month's latest title plus an earlier title from the Hard Case Crime archives. I'll get to preview each month's titles for 10 days. If I decide to keep them, I will pay only $6.99* each month — a savings of 50%! There is no minimum number of books I must buy and I may cancel my membership at any time.

Name: _____

Address: _____

City / State / ZIP: _____

Telephone: _____

E-Mail: _____

☐ **I want to pay by credit card:** ☐ VISA ☐ MasterCard ☐ Discover

Card #: _____ Exp. date: _____

Signature: _____

Mail this card to:
HARD CASE CRIME BOOK CLUB
20 Academy Street, Norwalk, CT 06850-4032

Or fax it to 610-995-9274.
You can also sign up online at www.dorchesterpub.com.

* Plus $2.00 for shipping. Offer open to residents of the U.S. and Canada only. Canadian residents please call 1-800-481-9191 for pricing information.

If you are under 18, a parent or guardian must sign. Terms, prices, and conditions subject to change. Subscription subject to acceptance. Dorchester Publishing reserves the right to reject any order or cancel any subscription.

He didn't notice the sidebar column in the *Breeze* until he sat down again at the computer. The column, running alongside the story about the library, carried the small headline NO DISPUTE BETWEEN US, and it had the local captain of detectives denying "rumors and more rumors" that McKinney was "interfering" with the investigation.

"We welcome," the captain was quoted as saying, "whatever help he—or anyone—can give us."

The story then went on to tell again, with a few details that were new for Alan, of the murder of McKinney's daughter: How he, his wife and two children—Sharon had been the youngest—had been supposed to leave for a week's vacation in Wildwood the day after she was killed, how she was involved in church charities and had often talked of wanting to be a nun.

Later that morning, in his office, he had the strangest thought about the Sharon McKinney Foundation. And what was even more inexplicable was that he didn't think it *was* strange, at least for a little while. So when he met with Elsa Tomlinson later on some matter, he said to her before leaving her office, and almost without planning to, "Do we ever help fund police work?"

"No. But tell me, such as?"

"I mean, like giving grants to help fund investigations into old cases, particularly involving children?"

"No. But do you have anything specific in mind?"

"Well, it's all vague at the moment."

"Well, when you think it out let me know."

By the time he got back to his office he was lashing himself. What was he trying to do?

Chapter Twenty-Three

It struck me as strange, after almost two weeks, that I still hadn't heard from Alan after I'd left a message on his answering machine congratulating him on his new position and asking him to call me back. When I called him one evening at his apartment he apologized, saying he'd been so busy that he kept putting it off. Please forgive him, he said.

"Absolutely," I said, "not. Anyway," and I laughed, "let me congratulate you again. How's it going?"

"Great. It's really going fine."

"Look, we haven't seen you for a long time. How about coming over for dinner? Patty says no, but I say yes."

He laughed. "When do you have in mind?"

"Any day I'm not here. Seriously, Saturday? Friday? Whenever's best for you."

"Can I bring someone?"

"Of course. So, let's make it Saturday if that's okay."

The following morning, at about half-past eight, I got a call from Haggerty, the editor of *Detective Eye*. This wasn't an unusual time for him; it meant that he'd been thinking about something half the night.

"Colin," he said, "this Harmann murder you got

down there. The Luder thing. From what I read here it's sewed up."

"All I know is that they arrested this guy and he's confessed."

"Look, talk to the cops. If they think it's sewed up, let's go with it. And this is important—I'll need it in eight days. The latest."

"Okay." But I almost groaned.

I was puzzled and disturbed by this. I'd heard that in the old days, when there were many true detective magazines, some of them routinely published cases before the suspect was even tried, in order to beat the competition. But it was a dangerous practice: If you labeled someone a killer and he or she was acquitted, it could mean quite a lawsuit. I wondered why Haggerty, without all that competition, would want to do it now, except that he must be low on stories as the deadline approached.

Patty came to the doorway of my office before leaving for work.

"Hey, what's with the long face?"

I told her. "It's bad enough that I hate doing these goddamn things but I really don't like being part of this one."

"Then just call him back and tell him how you feel."

"Yeah."

"Yeah what?"

"Yeah, there's a million other guys who'll do it in a second. And that'll be the end of me for anything else from him."

"So?"

"So, it's a problem." I took a deep breath. "Look, I'll think it over."

"You just call him. Please. You don't have to do this." She came over to my chair and kissed me on the cheek. "Honey, I have a job. Remember that. It doesn't pay an awful lot but it pays. And something's going to break for you. I know it. And I think you know it too. So you don't have to do this."

I smiled at her and we kissed, this time on the lips. She looked at me from the doorway and raised her thumb. I raised mine back at her, and we both smiled.

I kept sitting at the desk, a frown forming soon after I heard the apartment door close behind her. Then, almost without thinking, I swept up the phone. I had to at least let Haggerty know where the case stood.

"Homicide," a voice said.

"Detective Murray, please." He was one of my many contacts.

"He's a little busy now, can he call you back?"

His call came through about an hour and a half later. "Colin, what can I do for you?"

"Joe, it's about the Harold Luder case. Do you think it's pretty much wrapped up?"

"Wrapped up? Oh God, man, no. It's just starting all over again. He says he's killed at least thirty girls up and down the East Coast before and after he went to prison. Christ, we've been getting calls from cops all over, from South Carolina way up to—well, way up to Cape Cod."

◦

If Alan showed any anxiety when he and Anna came to our apartment, neither Patty nor I noticed it. I had expected Anna to be pretty but for some reason I didn't expect her warmth. She stood with Patty in the kitchen while Patty was putting some last touches together, and after dinner helped clear the table. She had a beautiful smile and, when prodded, spoke about her work in a way that made us feel she had to be an angel. And she looked at Alan in a way that, when Patty and I spoke about it later, warmed the both of us. He was forever smiling at her.

When they left, Patty said, "I think she's great, I think she would be marvelous for him. He'd be mighty lucky to have her."

"Do you still say he has sad eyes?"

"Oh," she said, drawing out the word, "not tonight. And especially not when he looked at her."

I felt equally good for Alan. And right before going to bed I thought of something that made me feel good for myself.

The Luder case. If it was true he killed all those girls, this could be the book I'd been hoping for.

Chapter Twenty-Four

About a half hour after Alan came home from the office that Monday he got a call from a man with a low voice. He didn't say hello, just, "Is this Mr. Benning?"

"Yes."

"This is Anna's father."

Alan was not only surprised he was calling but that he called him Mr. Benning—until he remembered vaguely that her father had never referred to him by any name during his visit.

"This is Alan, yes. How are you?"

He ignored the question. "I'm just calling to find out what goes with you and my daughter."

Alan shut his eyes for a moment. "Well, we're... seeing each other."

"I know, I know that. I mean, do you intend on getting married?"

Oh God. He managed to say, "Have you talked to Anna about it?"

"No, I can't always get things out of her. I'm talking to you."

"Well, we're seeing each other." Which was so damn dumb.

"I know you're seeing each other. Do you intend getting married?"

"We really haven't talked about it."

There was silence for a long moment. Then an angry, "I don't want her hurt."

"I'm not out to hurt her, Mr. Presiac."

"I don't want her hurt," he repeated, as if he didn't know what else to say.

"I wouldn't hurt her. I would never hurt her." Oh Christ!

"There are too many bums around. I'm sick and tired of bums. And Anna doesn't deserve bums."

Alan didn't say anything; couldn't think of anything *to* say. Nor apparently could her father.

"I just want you to know," her father said.

And with that he hung up, but it was a moment or two before Alan put down the phone. He couldn't even begin to blame the guy; he'd obviously seen a few bums in her life. But what could Alan tell him? God, he loved Anna, but how could he marry her? He couldn't tell her what he'd done; at the same time, he couldn't make a secret murderer a part of her life. And it was with a great hollowness through him that he knew what he'd really known all along, that he had to give her up.

Anna was coming over after work; he had said he would make dinner, and he'd bought steaks and a number of other things on his way home. But when she walked in and they kissed, she sensed something. "Is anything wrong?"

"No." He wasn't going to tell her about the call. She was aggravated enough about her sister.

"You look like you've had a hard day."

"No, it really wasn't. It was fine."

He made dinner, with her standing by in the kitchen and helping out. Afterward, as they were cleaning up, the phone rang. A woman identified herself as a Mrs. Beecher.

"I'm one of the nurses at your mother's nursing home." She paused and he was sure his mother was dead. But then she said, "Your mother, I wish you would do something. She's carrying on terribly, she hit another patient, she slapped a nurse when we tried talking to her. Nothing's working, she's got the strength of a—of a mule. We're afraid she's going to fall, break something, her hip—"

"I'll be right over."

When he told Anna she asked if she could go with him. He said, "God, you have enough of nursing homes."

"I'd like to if you'd let me."

His mother was sitting on the side of her bed, her arms folded around her bosom. She was shaking slightly. A nurse was bending over her, an aide was standing by. Her roommate in the next bed was sitting up, staring straight ahead.

"Mom." He kneeled in front of her. "It's me. It's Alan."

She kept quivering, was looking past him.

"Mom, it's Alan," he said again.

He took one of her hands and though it was rigid at first it gradually relaxed; she let him hold it, but she was still looking away.

"It's all about her comb," the nurse said to him. "She keeps saying Mary here"—the roommate—"stole it. She must have lost her comb, maybe down the toilet, and now she's blaming—"

"Did you look through Mary's things?" he asked her.

"Of course we did," she answered, annoyed.

"Patients," Anna said, "sometimes hide things in the weirdest places."

"We've looked all over," the nurse retorted. But then, as if to prove it, she started going through the roommate's night table and bureau. And after a few minutes she said, "Oh my. We actually looked here before." And she held up the comb, which she found in a tangle of Mary's nightgowns.

His mother seemed to go limp when it was handed to her.

"Would you like to lie down now?" Alan asked her.

She said nothing but let him ease her down on the bed and cover her with a thin blanket.

"Mom," he said, "I'd like you to meet a friend of mine. This is Anna."

She looked at Anna. And when Anna took her hand, he saw a smile—a thin one, barely perceptible but a smile. And something immediately struck him.

In all these years, Anna was the first girlfriend of his that his mother had ever met.

When he parked in front of Anna's building, she quickly put her hand out to stop him from getting out of the car with her.

"Honey," she apologized, "let's say goodnight here. I'm sorry but I'm really beat."

"Okay." But it was obvious that something was troubling her, perhaps something she'd been holding in all evening.

She just sat there for a moment, looking at her handbag on her lap. Then without looking up, "My father called you, didn't he?"

"Yes."

She looked at him. "I was waiting for you to tell me. You weren't going to, though, were you?"

"No. I knew it would upset you."

She nodded quickly. Then tears formed on her eyes. "I'm so upset. I'm so angry at them, at my father, my sister."

"Who told you?"

"My sister. She couldn't wait to call and tell me. It was like ha ha. Oh Alan, I'm so sorry. I feel like such a baby, such a shit."

He put his arm around her but her face was turned away from him. He told himself you're going to break up with her, you must, you will drive her crazy, you have to do it, let it start now. But instead he said, trying to bring her closer, "Honey, don't. It's not worth this."

"But I'm so angry. I feel so embarrassed."

"Don't, please don't." And almost against his will, though he wanted this so badly, he held her even tighter, his cheek against her hair.

"You're not sorry," she said, "you met me, are you?"

"Are you kidding?"

They walked hand in hand up the steps to the doorway. Two women, tenants, were standing there as one of them was working her key in the lock. When she had the door open, she joined the other in looking at them, and both smiled.

"I think," Anna whispered, smiling, as the women walked far ahead to their apartment, "they approve."

"I've been holding my breath."

Closing the door to her apartment, she put her arms around his neck. They kissed, his fingers under her hair, pressing her to him. She drew back soon. "Honey, do you mind if I shower?"

"Yes, I like you sweaty and dirty."

She laughed and gave him a quick little kiss.

The water had barely started running in the stall shower when he tapped against the misty door.

"I've got your mail," he said. "It just came."

"This late?"

"It's special delivery. You have to sign for it."

"Oh? Do you have a pen?"

"Do I have a pen," he said.

She opened the door and he stepped in. The water was just hot enough. She looked up at him, the water draining down her face, and he circled her with his arms and kissed her, deep. A look of surprise crossed her face as he lifted her up to his waist but then her legs quickly closed around him. He held her back against the wall.

"Oh darling Alan I love you."

"And I love you."

She held onto him even tighter, her face against his shoulder. And later, her body sagging, she slid down from him, their arms still holding each other, her face against his chest. In bed, his arm over her, they fell asleep within minutes of each other.

In the morning they were having breakfast when she said quickly, "Oh let me get the paper for you," and she started to go out to the hall for it.

"No, don't. Don't. You don't have to."

"No trouble at all. And sometimes, I hate to say it, sometimes it gets stolen."

She came back, looking at the front page, and then put the paper next to him on the table and went over to the sink to get more coffee. He looked over at it and in a first fast glance saw nothing of interest to him. Until, moments later, he saw it.

The sketch of his face on the front page.

Chapter Twenty-Five

Panicked, he folded the paper quickly and kept it by him, praying she wouldn't ask to see it, trying to think what he would say if she did, sure that his face must be ashen, that something about him would give his panic away. But she just asked if he would like more coffee.

"No, this is fine." He was fighting to keep a tremor out of his voice.

"I'm telling you," she said with a smile, "you really scared me last night."

"Really? I don't know why." He was trying to act as if he were kidding but he wasn't; his brain was in such tumult that for a few seconds he had no idea what she was talking about.

"You don't know why," she repeated, smiling. Then she reached over and took his hand. "Beating on the shower door like you did?"

"Ah, did you enjoy the shower?" And he tried, even, to force a smile.

"Oh, I loved the"—she paused before the word—"shower."

A little later, as they were starting to leave the apartment, he said, holding the folded paper, "Do you mind if I take this with me? There's something I want to see."

"Take it. I'll talk to you later." She lifted her face and he kissed her.

In the car, he pulled open the paper. The sketch, a small one, was one of several items that filled a column called Nationwide that ran on the left of the front page; each item listed a page number for the full story on the inside. Quickly he went to the third page. There the sketch was twice as large; the story, by the Associated Press, ran four or five paragraphs.

Although it was relatively short he had to try reading it a couple of times before he could calm down enough to get through it. There was nothing in it he didn't know: It gave a brief history of the "fifteen-year-old mystery," and reported on the "routine" search for the visitor to the library. But now it would be in papers throughout the country, and everyone would know.

He had to run, he told himself. He didn't know where but he had to pack a few things and just run. Or give himself up. Or kill himself. But where could he run to that would be safe? And give himself up? He was terrified of that, even more than of killing himself. And he couldn't see killing himself—unless he was cornered, had a gun, raised it to his head in blind fear and no longer caring.

One thing he was sure of was that his life in this city, or any other for that matter, was over. That sketch— Anna would see it, everyone at work would see it, all the people in his building would see it, the nurses in his mother's nursing home would see it, people he

passed on the street would see it; maybe even the desk
clerk back at that hotel who had his name and address.
So he couldn't go to work, couldn't live in his apartment anymore, would never feel safe enough to go
into a store to buy something, couldn't even buy gas
for his car without risk.

He kept touching his mouth, trying to think.

All he could come up with was that he had to
buy time, see what developed and who suspected
what, before he did anything he could never undo. He
thought: I'll call in sick and just wait and see. But wait
and see what? And wouldn't his not showing up for
work on the day the sketch appeared confirm that it
was really him?

But how could he just walk into that place with
those dozens of eyes?

He started the car and began driving in the direction of the office though still trying to decide what to
do. He was still debating it in his head as he drove
along the street leading to the parking lot near his
building. And he was still agonizing over a decision as
he approached the lot.

He turned into it, almost as if with closed eyes.

He stood with a group of people waiting at the elevators. A couple of them were reading newspapers,
but most were standing with their eyes fixed on the
elevator doors. He didn't recognize anyone from the
Foundation.

The elevator opened directly to the Foundation's
large reception room before closing and continuing

up. He nodded good morning to the young woman at the desk, then started his long walk past people at their desks or in their offices.

"Good morning, Mr. Benning," from a secretary he had never spoken to.

"Good morning."

"Lunch today?" It was Bob Feingold, a fellow about his own age who worked directly under him, standing in the doorway to his office.

"Okay." Then regretted it instantly. To go out to a crowded restaurant when he didn't have to?

"Hello." Someone else.

"Hello."

And his secretary: "Good morning."

"Good morning."

In his office he sagged onto his chair. There were letters on the desk his secretary had opened and put there. It took a while to settle himself down enough to read a couple of them, both appeals for grants, then almost jumped in alarm when his intercom buzzed.

"Alan, are you free for me?" It was Elsa Tomlinson.

"Yes, I am." He pulled in a breath and walked to her office.

"I'd like your thoughts on this," she said, holding up a sheaf of papers.

It had to do, she explained, with some programs for which a private high school in Montana was seeking funding. They talked of other things, grants, proposals, the direction she thought the Foundation should be taking in the near future. Then, as he was ready to leave, she said, "Oh, about that funding in child crime you spoke about, that could be very worthwhile. Could you write up something more about it for me?"

"Yes," but thinking: Maybe someday.

Back in his office he just wanted to close his eyes and sleep forever. But he managed to do some work. Then, about an hour later, while he was trying to read through a proposal, a voice at his doorway said:

"Hey, I see you made the newspaper."

He looked up sharply, a scalding going through him.

It was Jameson, the vice president with the bowtie. He was holding up the paper. Then his face reddened.

"I'm sorry," he apologized. "Bad joke."

"I don't know what you mean."

"Oh, a bad joke," he apologized again. "But there was a funny resemblance with something in the paper. Sorry to have interrupted you."

After Jameson walked off, he just sat there, numb except for the beating of his heart. How long could he get away with this? God, for how long?

Bob Feingold came by next. "Ready for lunch?"

Alan looked at him from his desk. "Oh. Look, I'm sorry, I really can't break away right now."

"Should I wait?"

"No, I probably will skip lunch."

"That, my friend, is setting a bad precedent."

But he smiled, gave Alan a thumbs-up and left.

As it turned out, he didn't have a reason to leave his office that afternoon. Then when it was time to go he waited for most of the other people to leave before going out to the elevator. Walking to the parking lot he felt a kind of release that he had made it through this day. And then he did something he knew was crazy. He turned around on the sidewalk and began walking against most of the flow of people leaving work. He looked at faces as they passed, and gave them a chance to get a good look at his. Then when he got back to the apartment house he said hello to the few people waiting for the elevator and looked squarely at each of them.

It was only when he was in his apartment, the door locked behind him, that he began to tremble.

Chapter Twenty-Six

He looked at his trembling hands and could hardly believe he had done that. What had it proved? It was totally insane.

Later that night, he got a phone call from Gregg Osterly.

"Hey, I want you to know your girlfriend made a big hit here. Especially," he laughed, "with me."

"Good."

"Only good? I just gave her the highest mark. Anyway, I want to know how about squash tomorrow?"

"I don't think I can tomorrow but let me call you."

"By the way, you know what made me think of you?" Gregg laughed. "There's a picture in the paper today of some guy, some witness or something, that reminded me of you."

Alan had been standing holding the phone. Now he slowly sat down with it.

"Did you see it?" Gregg asked.

"I don't know what you're talking about."

"It's one of those police sketches. Well, it doesn't look all that much like you, but I got a kick out of it. Anyway, buddy, call me tomorrow."

Putting the phone down, Alan just stared at it. Only then was he aware of how his heart was hammering.

He tried to take comfort in the fact that only two people he knew—at least so far—had seen even the vaguest resemblance between that sketch and him. But what of people he didn't know about who might have quietly phoned in tips?

Again he felt everything closing in on him.

He was back once more to giving himself up. And he tried to find hope in it. The police knew he hadn't raped her: They said it, and that would be in his favor, wouldn't it? But they also thought it had been her father calling to her that had stopped it; and even though that wasn't true, he *had* touched her, touched her…there. And more than once. Twice. That meant he would go into the deepest prison hell not only as a murderer but a sexual predator.

Again he was back to thinking of suicide—but this time as a comfort, something he could do if he decided to in desperation. But how? Overdose on pills? But he didn't know what kind he'd need or how to get them. Plow his car into a tree? Use a gun? But he didn't have a gun.

He pulled out the phone book, opened it quickly and found that there was a gun shop only two blocks from his office. He closed the book slowly.

He felt a little comfort already.

Going into his office in the morning was as hard for him as it had been the day before. After all, many people didn't read the newspaper until they got home from work. Calls might have been exchanged between people here: *Hon, look at that picture, doesn't it look like...?* Or perhaps just looking at him today, even in passing, might stir up a connection.

The main part of the morning was taken up with a meeting with Mrs. Tomlinson and a few others. New projects were discussed, some rejected, others delayed for further study, just one accepted. He was hoping she wouldn't bring up the child-crime funding possibility, for he had nothing more to say on it, not even the vaguest thought on following through; and she didn't.

About a quarter to one, during lunch hour, he was walking to the gun shop.

He remembered how as a kid he used to want a BB rifle. But he never even bothered to ask his parents for one. Lose an eye? Hurt someone? Are you kidding? He knew those answers without even hearing them— because he'd heard similar ones about other things. But Tommy next door, who was only a year older, had one. And not only did Tommy have one, Tommy's father and two brothers were hunters, and they had a cabinet filled with rifles, and several walls in their home were hung with deer heads. It was a bad day for Tommy when he didn't kill a sparrow perched high on a telephone wire or tree limb. The neighborhood seemed to take this with a casual, "Oh, that's Tommy." On this one day Alan was with him behind their houses when they saw a blackbird standing a few yards ahead of them on the grass. Tommy handed him his rifle and, almost without thinking, Alan aimed and fired, and to his horror the bird actually flopped over, and he was running back into his house in disbelief and fear. But a mother had witnessed it from her window, and a funeral was held, attended by most of the kids around there, perhaps including Tommy. No one was allowed to speak to Alan for a week.

"Maybe you'll learn," his mother said. "I hope so."

"I would never have expected that of you," his father said.

Now he was at the gun shop, trying to buy something he'd never once handled. A grandmotherly woman was behind the counter.

"I'm interested in buying a handgun. For protection," he added.

He had this feeling that she would at least look at him strangely. But she simply said, "Do you know what you want?"

"No, I'd appreciate you showing me some."

She brought several models over to the counter and he selected a .22 Smith and Wesson, simply because it was the name he was most familiar with. He had to give her his driver's license and fill out a form stating among other things that he had no criminal record. The computerized check of the information was finished quickly. And half an hour later he was walking back into the offices of the Elsa and Jonathan Tomlinson Foundation, hub of so much great and important work, holding an unmarked blue plastic bag, in it a package containing his Smith and Wesson and a small box of shells. He hid it temporarily deep in his file cabinet, behind a row of folders.

In his apartment he had to decide again where to put it. He wanted it someplace where he could grab it at the first suspicious sound at his door, hold it ready in his hand and at the sight of a cop put it to his temple and just squeeze the trigger. But what if it happened outside, if they started to close around him on the sidewalk? Should he carry it in his pocket? Get a license for that?

He started to put the gun and shells in one drawer, then another, but still had them in his hands. No place seemed quite right.

It was strange, but if anyone was going to catch up with him he saw it being McKinney. He pictured him pursuing every lead, every hint of a clue, until it led here. He saw McKinney following him in his car as he walked along the sidewalk. He saw him at his door, ringing the bell and saying "package." He saw him clearing everyone away at the Foundation and waiting just outside his office. He saw him kicking in the door to his apartment—and, in a blaze of desperation, saw himself grabbing hold of his gun and firing bullet after bullet into him.

Firing and firing—

He touched his head in horror at himself.

Me? *Me?* The killer in him he feared?

All he knew now was that he *must* get rid of the gun, not just put it away in the apartment. But where? In the trash? The river? Dig a hole somewhere and bury it? But it was as if there was no place in this world where it was safe enough—from him.

Chapter Twenty-Seven

That morning I saw the sketch when I looked at the paper at breakfast. At first it meant nothing to me, and then when I noticed the resemblance it struck me as funny. I showed it to Patty.

"Who does this remind you of?"

She looked at it carefully, then at me, puzzled. "Who?"

"You don't see it?"

"I see a drawing, that's all. Who?"

"Never mind." I smiled and put down the paper.

"Tell me, who?"

"Oh, nothing. I thought it looked a little like my cousin, that's all."

"Alan?" She picked up the paper again. She looked at the sketch once more, head tilted. "Maybe. Maybe just a little." Then, shaking her head, "No, I really don't see it."

"I just thought it was funny," I said, and she put aside the paper.

I didn't read the paper until I was at my desk. And I didn't get to that story until I read the ones I was really interested in as well as the op-ed page. Then I looked at the larger sketch on the third page but this time it was just that, a sketch of someone or other. And the story of

Susheela Kapasi's murder was like so many others—
until the name South Minton registered with me.

This, Detective Murray had told me, was one of the
murders Harold Luder may have committed.

I could kill again.

That's what he told himself, almost in disbelief.

But believe it, he told himself. *Believe it, believe it.*

After checking off in his mind every possible hiding
place in the apartment, Alan gave in to terror and put
the gun in what seemed like the most practical one,
the top drawer of his night table, where it would be in
quick reach should he hear sounds in the night.
Though he still tried assuring himself he would never
use it on anyone else, it was becoming a comfort again
just knowing it was there.

Sitting at his computer it took him just a few minutes to confirm what he had already assumed: that the
sketch and Associated Press story were in newspapers
throughout the country. But actually seeing it made it
new, made it even more devastating.

There was nothing in the stories themselves that he
hadn't read before. But he had only checked under the
name "Susheela Kapasi" and now he typed in "Mack
McKinney." This time there was even more about him
than Alan had known. He had enlisted for Vietnam
when he didn't have to, was awarded the Silver Star,
was a deacon in his church, had been shot and almost
killed while making an arrest, did volunteer work in a
hospital—

He turned off the computer.

He'd found that he was thinking of McKinney more than ever as a human being. And he had to think of him, must think of him—and all cops—as his enemy.

That evening he took Anna to a Thai restaurant he'd heard good things about, and afterward, as they started to drive back to her place in the clear evening light, he said, "You know, we're not far from where I grew up."

"Really?"

"Honest. You can look it up in the history books."

"You are funny. Can we go see?"

"You do know what to say, don't you?" It was amazing, he thought, how almost light-hearted he could become with her.

He didn't know why, but he suddenly wanted to show it to her, the house and the neighborhood where he'd lived before they moved to the suburbs.

They drove slowly through the neighborhood, stopping now and then at places that had been so important to him. He pointed out the windows of his old bedroom, showed her where the kids would play ball, even the approximate spot where he'd shot the blackbird. He showed her my old place, too, and explained how we'd just about lived in each other's houses. And over there was the house where the first kid about his own age died, a boy of eight who had what was thought to be a cold and simply died. But no, he said quickly, he was wrong: That was the second death. The first had

been Eddie, a kid who had been in the second grade
with him and who'd been killed by a truck when he ran
into the street after a ball.

"For years," he said, "I'd see his mother walking
around the neighborhood all alone. She seemed like a
ghost."

Over here, some ten blocks away, was his old
grammar school, and close by were the woods and
creek where Will Jansen and he would play Tarzan and
where his mother would occasionally come looking to
make sure he hadn't drowned. And where she once
caught them sitting back against a large rock smoking
cigarettes and looking up at the sky.

It was only when they were driving away that he
became aware that it wasn't so much that he had
wanted Anna to see his old house and neighborhood.
That was a big part of it, to be sure. But most of all, he
thought, he'd wanted to feel, even for just the short
time they were there, all that innocence again.

In bed that night, with Anna asleep next to him, he
thought about that innocence.

He had read somewhere that serial killers, or
maybe every kind of ruthless killer, showed signs of
cruelty in childhood, such as torturing animals. One of
the things he remembered that fit in was the time an
elderly woman who lived close by called to Will Jansen
and Alan as they were walking by her house. They
were no more than eight at the time.

"Would you boys do me a big favor?"

She was a woman they were sort of afraid of, since she had what they looked on as a witch's face, and lived alone in a large house and was rarely seen.

"I got this cat that's gone crazy," she said. "I called the police yesterday and once today and they're still not here. I'm an old woman and I need help, would you help me get rid of it? Please?"

She pointed to a covered basket from which they could hear screeches and scratching.

"Just drop it in the creek for me, that's all, will you? It'll be an act of mercy."

He and Will looked at each other. He ached to say no but didn't know how to say it to an old woman. And he guessed that Will didn't either.

"Go on. Please, boys, go on."

He and Will each took hold of a handle and carried the shaking, screeching basket to the woods. There they quickly set it down among the trees—not in the creek—and ran back as though running from ghosts.

Then there was the time a couple of years later when he and Will were playing in the garage attached to Alan's house. A boy from a couple of streets away, just a year or so younger than they, appeared in the doorway. He was "slow," and so when they closed the door behind him and said he was their prisoner and would never see his mother and father again he believed it. The only way they would let him go, they told him, was if he would go to Haines's grocery store, about a block away, and ask for "pigeon milk."

Oh, Alan recalled, what a laugh they'd had as he walked off.

But what troubled him most of all, now, was that it had been his idea, not Will's.

Chapter Twenty-Eight

Sam Haggerty called me a week later while Detective Murray was sitting with me at my desk, to ask with a sound of desperation in his voice if I saw any "daylight" in the "Harmann case," which was his way of asking when did I think I could write it.

"No, and I'm afraid I won't anytime soon," I told him. "Like I said, the case is still very wide open."

"Well, have you got anything else for me?" he demanded, annoyed. "You know I need copy."

"I really haven't seen anything that strikes me as that good."

"You haven't seen anything?" he repeated, sudden anger in his voice. "Hell, maybe you're reading different papers than I am."

And he rattled off two crimes in western Pennsylvania and one in New Jersey. "Have you checked on any of them?"

"No, but I will."

"Listen, if you're not interested any more or you're too busy, tell me. Just tell me."

"I would, but it's not so." I glanced over at Murray, as if he could hear Haggerty's voice.

"All right then," and with that he hung up.

I was angry as I put down the phone, not so much at

him as at myself, that I was still back—even for a little while—to writing that crap. I looked at Detective Murray.

Harold Luder had led police to the gravesites of two more of his victims, one a girl of nine, the other a girl of fifteen, both of whom had been missing for years.

"He's told the truth about three murders so far," he said, "but he's beginning to confess to so many things we don't know yet which if any of it is full of crap."

It was either that same morning or the next, as I try to piece it all together, that a few things fell into place that led Alan to take a subway instead of driving to work.

One was that he needed to take his car to the dealer's for some work that had to be done. He had made the appointment a couple of weeks earlier. The second was that the place was several miles from his office and he didn't feel like waiting the half hour or so for the dealer's van to take him and several others downtown. And a subway entrance was right outside.

So, at the same time that a certain stranger was standing somewhere near him, he was waiting on the platform for a subway he hadn't been on in several years.

Standing there among a crowd of people waiting for the train, he was suddenly angry at himself for not having taken a cab, for having let himself forget that someone could still identify him from the sketch. So he didn't look at any faces, never noticed anyone in particular, just kept looking down the tracks for the first sound and sign of the train. It was only as the train made the turn far down the tracks and came roaring toward the station that something caught his attention to his left.

In a blur of motion a man next to him took a fast step across the yellow warning line on the platform, started to spring onto the tracks, and somehow, instinctively, both of Alan's hands were on him, straining to pull him back. And now his arms were completely around the man, for he was struggling to get loose and was pulling Alan out with him; and now they were stumbling around on the platform together as the cars rumbled and clanked past them and then came to a stop.

The fellow tore free, and after a few swings at Alan he ran through the startled crowd and, from what Alan was to hear, up the stairs to the street.

Alan spent a minute or two just sitting on the platform, trying to clear his head, a man's voice asking, "Are you hurt, are you okay?"

He remembered nodding and the voice saying, "You mean you're hurt? You want an ambulance?"

"No, I'm okay."

"You sure?"

And Alan was nodding again, and then another voice, a woman's, was saying, "What a crazy, he almost killed you!"

Alan stood up, aware that what he'd thought was a crowd around him was only two or three people, that everyone else had boarded the train and was gone.

Then within a few moments a cop materialized. Someone had apparently told him about the incident and sent him running here.

"How're you doing there, buddy?"

"I'm okay."

"You've got a bruise on your face. Maybe you ought to go to an emergency room."

Alan touched his cheek. "No, I'll be okay, I'm all right."

"What happened, you tried to stop him from jumping and he fought you?"

Alan nodded. "It just happened so fast."

"Do you know the guy?"

"No."

"Anyone here know the guy?" He turned to the others. But apparently no one did. Then back to Alan: "Did you get a good look at him?"

"No, it happened so fast. All I'm sure of is he had black hair."

"Was he white? Black?"

"I think white."

"Latino?"

"I don't know."

"Anyone know?" The cop looked around.

One man said definitely white—although he, too, hadn't gotten a look at the man's face—and that he was "like" in his late thirties or maybe early forties, which Alan had the feeling might be right.

The cop took out a pad and said to him, "Let me have your name."

"It's ok, I'm all right."

"This isn't for you, buddy, it's for me."

"Alan Benning."

"And your address."

For a few moments Alan found that he couldn't think of his own address. Maybe it was brain-freeze brought on by this uniformed cop standing there questioning him. Or maybe it was aftershock. But the only thing he could think to say was, "I'm with the Tomlinson Foundation," and when the cop asked where that was that's when Alan's address came back to him and he gave it to him.

The first thing Alan did when he got to the office was go to the men's room. He had a large welt on his left cheek. It hadn't hurt before but it was tender now. One of the secretaries noticed it as he walked by her desk, and she looked about to say something but didn't. Ron Jameson frowned and then gave a slight smile above his bowtie.

"What happened to you, friend?"

"Just a stupid accident."

"And the other guy?"

"He's probably answering the same questions I am."

Elsa Tomlinson's face showed concern when he went to her office later with some papers that needed her signature.

"How did you ever do that?"

"It was just an accident. It's fine. I ran into somebody's elbow."

"Somebody's *elbow?*" she repeated.

"I took a subway here, and there was a crowd and I got in the way of an elbow."

She looked at him curiously.

"I was not in a bar fight," he told her, managing a smile.

He didn't know if that reassured her. But the next morning was totally different. He had looked through the newspaper before leaving for work without seeing anything about the incident—not that he really expected to—but when he approached his office his secretary smiled at him from her desk and said, "Congratulations."

"For what?"

"Did you see this?" She held up the newspaper. And his heart started to sink.

She stood up and opened it to one of the back pages and handed it to him, smiling. Then she pointed to a popular local gossip column, Sid's Place, which he hadn't even thought to look at. He scanned it quickly.

> Sid's agents tell him that Alan Benning, senior vice president of the Elsa and Jonathan Tomlinson Foundation, did a bit of "charity work" that was, sadly, under-appreciated to say the least. Alan stopped a stranger from jumping in front of a subway train—and received punches in "gratitude" from the man, who then ran away. Alan, we—if not a certain ingrate—honor you...

By now several other secretaries were smiling at

him from their desks. He couldn't wait to go behind his own desk.

Just a few minutes later Elsa Tomlinson was smiling at him from the doorway.

"You are one modest fellow, aren't you?"

"Elsa, I really didn't do anything."

"Oh yes. I know all about that. How's your face?"

"I'm fine, everything's fine."

"Well, I'm proud of you. Okay?" And she nodded, as if stamping it with her signature.

Later that day he got a call from a woman who identified herself as "Melanie Hollins from the *Toby Miller Show*."

"From where?" He was so startled that he said it even though he knew the name: It was one of the morning cable shows.

"From the *Toby Miller Show*. I'm an assistant producer. We heard about your experience in the subway yesterday and we think it will make an interesting short conversation with Toby. You wouldn't have to come to New York, we would—"

"No," he interrupted, "I appreciate it but I'd rather not."

His face all over the country?

"Really? Oh, why not? The rescuer becoming a victim—"

"Look, I did nothing great. I didn't even mean to do it. It's just something that happened."

"Oh, come on."

"I mean it. I'd rather not."

He had just about calmed down about the call when Elsa was in his office. She looked annoyed even before she spoke.

"You turned down a national interview? I can't believe it."

"Elsa, it didn't deserve it." He was getting tired of saying it. "I really didn't do anything."

"Didn't *do* anything. You know, you really don't have to save the world to do something good. The *Toby Miller Show*. I don't believe this."

And now he knew that her public relations people had set it up.

Chapter Twenty-Nine

When he came home he found one message and two hang-ups on his machine. The message was from me. It started off with something very clever, like, "Alan, when did you start using the subway? Seriously, that guy's got to be a nut. Anyway, I want you to know that Patty, Mom and I are so proud of you."

Anna called a few minutes later.

"Oh, honey, someone at work showed me the article just as I was about to leave. She'd heard me mention your name and wanted to know if it was you. I couldn't believe my eyes. I'm so proud of you. But what an awful thing he did to you."

"It wasn't all that bad, believe me."

"But to attack you—that was terrible. He must really be crazy."

"Probably."

"You know who needs to see this? My father. I can't wait to call home, in fact I'm going to send them the clipping."

Almost immediately afterward he got another call, this one from Gregg Osterly.

"Well, well, well, whatever happened?" he joked. "How *did* it happen? Now, the truth. Did you trip and stumble over him?"

"Damn, you must have been there."

"And for this they give you the key to the city?"

"Not even to the men's room."

He laughed. "Well, congratulations, buddy. Keep it up and one day I'm going to be proud to know you."

He appreciated the levity. The full impact of the incident hadn't hit him until he'd gotten to the office, and it was still with him: How someone standing on that platform, surrounded by people who were thinking only of getting to work or were reading their newspapers, had wanted to die and was willing to die so horribly. What had driven him to it? Had he planned it or had it been a sudden impulse? Alan couldn't help wondering, and wishing he knew. It seemed so damn lonely and sad.

He was angry at Elsa for trying to use it as a publicity gimmick. He had no illusions about charity as a business but this was so bald, so stupid. And, again, it wasn't as if he had really done something brave or thought-out. It had happened; he'd simply reacted.

A little later, driving to Anna's place, he found himself thinking of something else. For the past couple of minutes, and almost without realizing it, he had been thinking that maybe if he gave himself up this incident would help him, would serve to let them know he was really a good person, someone who deserved forgiveness, mercy. But then he remembered stories he'd read or heard about of killers sent away for life despite years of freedom living honorable lives.

*

The two of them weren't particularly hungry, so they decided on something less than a full meal for dinner. They drove to a Jewish delicatessen about a mile away and took the booth the farthest from the counter. The evening started off well, but as it wore on he could tell that she was tired, and by the time he drove her home they both felt, without saying it to each other, that this was not a night for him to stay over.

The red light on his answering machine was on when he walked in, but it was just another hang-up. He went in the bathroom and started to undress, changed his mind, then went to the computer.

He had put the link to the *Breeze* directly on his computer's desktop so that he could log onto the paper's Web site immediately. He opened it but after a fast scan saw nothing about his crime. Like a million times before, he told himself to stop but instead he went back to older articles archived below today's headlines. And saw that the sketch was still there, just a click away from the home page.

He forced himself to read the story, saw that the first few paragraphs were once again about the stranger in the library. But then something new: The local police were anxious to question a man who'd been arrested in Philadelphia for the murder of an eleven-year-old girl but who might be responsible for at least twenty other murders along the East Coast.

He sat back as though in a daze.

Although the thought horrified him, he saw this as hope.

And then it stopped horrifying him.

He must have been sitting there for at least five minutes, staring at the computer, when the phone rang. He just let it ring, waiting for the answering machine to take it. It stopped after three rings and the machine went on, and the silence that followed told him it was going to be another hang-up. Somehow this brought him out of it and he lifted the phone.

"Yes."

He got only silence. But he thought he could hear the sound of breathing.

"Hello," he said.

And this time a man's voice spoke. He said only one word. "Why?"

Alan frowned. "Who is this? Why what?"

"Why?" the man repeated. And his voice, which had been soft at first, was a little stronger.

"Who is this? Who are you?" Alan was about to hang up but then he heard:

"I didn't ask you to save me. I didn't want it. *Why?*" It was a shout now.

Alan's hand was frozen on the receiver.

"Was it any of your business?" the voice went on. "Any of your goddamn business? You wanted to be a big man, didn't you, a hero! Big shot! Get your name in the paper! Well, you got your name in the paper all right, you bastard!"

"I wasn't trying to be a hero," he shouted back. "I didn't even—I just did it!"

"Weren't trying to be a hero! Oh yeah! Well, fuck you! You hear me? Fuck you!"

And then the line went dead.

Chapter Thirty

He stood gripping the phone for several moments before putting it down. Then he tried to redial the number from which the call had come. Instead of ringing, he heard a recording: *We're sorry, but this payphone does not accept incoming calls.* He hung up.

What was going on? It was no mystery how the guy had gotten his home number—his name was right there in the damn phone book—but what did he want? He had to be a nut, a lunatic. He wanted to kill himself? Well, it wasn't as if, having been stopped once, he could never try again. He could still jump off a bridge or out a window or under another subway car, if that's really how he wanted to go.

As he gradually calmed down, Alan thought of the revolver and shells in his night table. It was as though the guy had called to say you're the last person in this world who should have stopped me. And maybe he was right.

Alan tried to put the call out of his mind. There were too many other things to think about, all of them infinitely more important. Like that guy Luger here in Philly. No, Luder. Luder. It was almost with a chill that he thought of him, and yet it was with something of relief, too.

But the following morning, driving to the office, every fear flooded back on him.

He had noticed a gray car pull out from the line of cars in back and then settle in right behind him. That was nothing, of course, but then he saw the same car—or was it?—follow him through a turn into another street, which still might be nothing but had him a little tense. His eyes kept going to the rear-view and side-view mirrors as he drove on. When he saw that the car was still behind him into another turn, he almost stood on the gas. He sped through a yellow light, then made several quick turns before feeling safe enough to pull into his parking lot.

His immediate thought was that it was the police in an unmarked car. But why? If they wanted to arrest or question him, they would simply do it. There was nothing he could think of that they would learn by following him around. His mind then went to that voice on the phone. But that was ridiculous, wasn't it? Why would *he* follow him when he knew where Alan lived and worked?

Walking along the crowded sidewalk to his building, he tried convincing himself it was all his imagination.

What was definitely not his imagination was Elsa Tomlinson's annoyance with him. She wasn't rude, they spoke about the usual business matters, but he could detect a difference. And then it came out, when she stopped him as he was leaving her office that afternoon.

"I just want to say this," she said. "I want you to

know I am quite proud of what you did."

"Thanks." But he waited for more.

"Nevertheless I think you were wrong in how you handled it. It's like you're ashamed. Or bashful. In business, in projects like ours, you can't be bashful, you know."

"I know what you're saying," he said. "But can I say this? Can I say this again? I don't want to act like the super-modest guy but I really didn't do anything heroic. It wasn't like I was brave, I just grabbed the guy."

"And that's nothing? All right, let's call it nothing if you want. It's more than something but let's call it nothing. There are too many lousy ways to get in the papers or on TV. And when a good way comes along that we're all proud of, I say take the opportunity. That's all."

He didn't say if he agreed with her or not. He just nodded again and went back to his office. He tried to lose himself in work but then as it grew time to leave he began to think more and more about Anna, how he had to stop seeing her. But when he got home and the phone rang and the first thing he heard was, "Alan, it's me. I want to see you, can I see you?" he almost ran to his car.

He was to doubt, later, whether he gave a thought to whether anyone was following him.

He came back to his apartment about seven in the morning, to shower and change before going to work, feeling a lightness that was almost strange in his life.

But the moment he walked in he saw the little light blinking on his answering machine, and when he went to listen it was as though the whole room was darkening around him. He heard only hang-ups, three of them. At least one if not all of them, he was sure, had to be *him.*

He took a shower but he couldn't help opening the shower door twice, thinking he might have heard the phone ringing. He was wrong each time. But he wasn't when it rang while he was dressing.

"You bastard," the same voice said.

"Look, what do you want?" It was almost a yell. "Tell me what you want!"

"What did you want from *me?* Tell me that. Why couldn't you leave me alone? Why didn't you leave me alone?"

"Let me tell you something. I'm sorry I did it. Okay? Okay? I'm sorry!"

"Sorry. You're sorry. You bastard, you have it so goddamn good," he went on, "you think everyone has it good! You don't know! You've got no idea!"

"I don't know? Who the hell says I have it good?"

"You're a goddamn lawyer. You've got money. You've got it all. And you think everyone has it all."

How, he wondered immediately, did this guy know he was a lawyer? The item in the paper hadn't said anything about that. But all he could think to say, in rage, was: "You bastard, you've been following me. It's you, isn't it? You know what? I should have let you die. What the hell do I care if you live or die?"

"And that's the goddamn truth! Finally the truth! You just don't know what suffering is, what real trouble is. You live in a world of your own. You've got no fucking idea."

"I don't? I don't? I don't know what suffering is? I don't know what trouble is?"

But then he caught himself and hung up fast.

He stood there, his hand holding down the phone.

My God, he thought. He had almost blurted it out.

Chapter Thirty-One

During this time I had my own tensions to deal with. The Luder case, I knew, had to be attracting every true crime writer in the country; and though I had alerted my publisher that I was looking into it, and he thought it worth following, I didn't have enough material yet for the kind of proposal that would bring not only a contract but a hefty advance.

And Haggerty, meanwhile, was still biting at my heels. Though he was starting to sound like he was ready to give up on me.

It wasn't that I hadn't accumulated material. In addition to talking with Detective Murray and a few other officers, I'd interviewed several of Luder's neighbors and a two of his nieces; his parents were dead, and a younger brother had died when Luder was ten. Although I had a long, long way to go, the picture of him that was emerging was so familiar as to be almost a cliché: The kid who was to grow up to be a serial murderer had been quiet, withdrawn, church-going, and an average student through high school. He then began drifting around, mostly working as a short-order cook, and had never been in any trouble until his arrest as a pedophile.

A story that, so far, had been told a million times.

I looked at the newspaper I had placed across my desk. Today's paper had a picture of Luder at still another gravesite, this one over in New Jersey. It showed him with some officers in the woods, staring down at what appeared to be a mound of leaves, his hands cuffed behind his back. Although he was clean-shaven there, the pictures at the time of his arrest had showed him with a straggly beard, half-bald, what hair he did have tied back in a gray ponytail.

I had just finished clipping out the picture and the story when I remembered something Patty had asked me to do that morning. She would be home soon and I still hadn't done it. I dialed Alan's number, and after a wait of several rings his voice came on, loud. "What do you want now? What do you want?"

Frowning, I held the phone away from my ear. Then, "Alan? What's wrong?"

Silence. A long one. "Oh God," his voice said quietly, "I'm sorry."

"I'm only trying to sell you an insurance policy," I said.

"I'm sorry, Colin. Oh Christ. I must have sounded like a horse's ass. But someone's been bugging me and I've had it."

"Is it your kindly minister's aged mother?"

He managed a little laugh. "It's just some guy bugging me, trying to sell me something."

"Well, with that you're forgiven."

And then I told him why I'd called: Patty and I

wanted to know if he and Anna would like to go out to dinner with us this Sunday.

"Sounds good but I'll let you know after I talk with her."

"Good enough. Take care. Oh by the way, don't be so shy with those guys."

He laughed again. A little one.

What I didn't know, of course, was that he had just gotten a call, where that voice said, "I want you to know—" and Alan had immediately hung up, wanting to throw the damn phone against the wall. And now, after my call to him, he remained standing by the phone although telling himself he wouldn't answer if it rang a thousand times.

But when the phone rang a few minutes later he couldn't resist and swept it up. But he just held it to his ear, said nothing.

"You're there," the voice said. "I know you're there. And I just want to say this."

"I'm right here," Alan said. "I'm right here. Now what the hell more do you want from me?"

"I just want to say this," he repeated, and for the first time Alan realized from the muffled tone of his voice that he must be holding something like a hand-kerchief to the mouthpiece. "I just want to say that you not only butted into something that was none of your business but you milked it, you got yourself publicity out of it."

"Look, you've said all this before. How many times do you want to say it?"

"Oh, you big hero," he went on, as if he hadn't heard. "Big man, big hero."

"Look, buddy, I didn't ask for that, I didn't want it."

"Oh you didn't want it! My ass. Let me ask you, do you know what being desperate means? Do you know what having nothing means? You have any idea at all?"

"Look, do you want me to call the police? Because that's what I'm going—"

"You can call whoever the hell you want. You can—"

Alan quickly put down the phone; set it down quietly, though he wanted to slam it back on its hook. His immediate thought was that, though he hated to, he would have to change to an unlisted phone number. But what good would that do since the guy knew where he worked and could call him there? He thought about calling the police, but that lasted only about five seconds. The last people he wanted to talk to were the police. The Cape Cod police had surely distributed the sketch to them, it was in their files, perhaps even in their memories. And anyway, they wouldn't get involved in tracking down nuisance calls. It wasn't as if he'd been threatened.

And yet he felt as if he were being threatened. And—though this seemed crazy—he had the eerie feeling there was a reason, a dark one, why the guy had come into his life.

That night he was concerned enough about the caller to think again about getting a license to carry a gun. The next morning he even called the shop where he'd bought the gun to see how long it would take to get one. Just a few days, he was told. But though he played with the idea of doing it, common sense said no: He was afraid he might use it. And for the next few days he had no reason to regret it.

Not only didn't he hear from the caller but the story of Susheela Kapasi disappeared again from the *Breeze*. No more sketch, no more about Luder. Alan wouldn't even let himself be bothered by the occasional thunder of music from next door.

That Sunday the four of us decided to go to the zoo before going to dinner. None of us had been there in years, and the fact that it was a cool gray day, with a possibility of rain, somehow made us even more interested in going: It wouldn't, we thought, be as crowded as usual. But it was, which didn't bother us at all. We ate popcorn as we walked along the paths through the outdoor exhibits. Many of the animals were indoors, perhaps sensing rain, and one of the exhibits we went to was the monkey house. And it was there that, without Patty and I being aware of it, Alan noticed a certain man.

Every time Alan glanced at him, the guy was looking at us but then would turn away.

He was standing at the fringe of the group gathered around the chimpanzee window. He looked to be in his mid-thirties and was rather short, with a round face, heavy-lidded eyes, and black hair that was brushed a little over his forehead, like bangs. He was wearing a light windbreaker, and from what Alan could see he also wore a nasty little smile. The four of us were about to walk on when Alan looked at him again, and this time the man's eyes didn't shift away. For a moment Alan felt a little jolt of recognition, even though he couldn't place him. But there seemed to be something, something....

Alan looked away. And then when he looked back he was gone.

Alan told himself that his imagination was out of control.

We all wanted to go to the carnivore house in time for the feeding of the lions and tigers. We had about twenty minutes to get there, and Anna, Patty and I went on ahead to get a good spot while Alan lingered behind to watch the monkeys a while longer. When he did enter the carnivore house it was echoing with roars as the animals, striding back and forth in their cages, anticipated the feeding.

This part of the building was jammed with people; it was the prime daily exhibition.

Alan looked around for us and then saw us at the back of the crowd; Anna, however, was turned away from the animals and was talking to that same man. Alan stood there watching. Then he walked a little closer. And it was then that the man saw him. He showed Alan, briefly, that same little smile, which seemed to have nothing of humor about it. Then he reached out and shook Anna's hand and started walking away, with a look over his shoulder at her.

Alan stood with us, forcing himself not to say anything as one of the keepers walked along the outside of the cages, flinging in slabs of red meat. But afterward, as the crowd thinned out, Alan said to her, "Who was that guy you were talking to?"

His voice was so sharp that Patty and I, who were just a little ahead, couldn't help turning quickly toward them.

"Who was who?" She looked genuinely puzzled. Then, "Oh, you mean that fellow."

"Yes, the guy you were talking with. Who is he?"

"Who is he? I don't know who he is. Just someone who started talking to me."

"Can I ask what about?" He didn't seem at all concerned that Patty and I were standing there, listening.

"Alan." She smiled. "Don't tell me you're jealous."

"I'm serious."

"What he talked to me about? About children. How the only way to really appreciate a zoo was to bring a child."

"I see."

"And how he remembered his aunt bringing him here. I guess she raised him. He said he felt bad because she has to go to a nursing home."

Alan felt a chill ripple through him. "He said that? He brought up nursing homes? Did you tell him you worked in one?"

"Alan, what is it?"

"I don't know. I'm not sure." He hadn't told her about the calls, hadn't wanted to worry her. And he wasn't sure if he should tell her now what he suspected.

"Alan, tell me what it is. You're starting to scare me."

I took Patty by the elbow and we walked a short distance away, to give them privacy. It was hardly subtle but I doubt if Anna or Alan noticed.

"Look," Alan said, "I don't know if this is so. I don't know for sure. But I have a feeling, I have a suspicion. A strong one. That he's the guy I pulled from the subway."

She stared at him, her mouth open. "Oh Alan, that can't be. Are you sure? It would be so coincidental."

"I said I don't know for sure. But I feel it, I think it."

"Oh this is so crazy." Then a look of anguish came over her face. "Alan, I didn't give him my name. But I did give him the name of the nursing home. Did I...oh Alan, was I wrong?"

Chapter Thirty-Two

It wasn't until they left us after dinner and had just gotten into their car that Alan decided to tell her about the calls. He'd been debating it in his head, hating to scare her but at the same time afraid for her. This guy at the zoo—and Alan was becoming convinced he was the caller—possibly had learned about Anna by following him to her place. If so, he not only was crazy, he was determined, and who knew what else he might do?

So he told her, and all the while she kept looking at him in dismay.

"Oh Alan, are you sure he's the one?"

"Like I told you, I'm not positive, I couldn't swear to it in court, but I'm almost positive."

"But wouldn't you recognize his face?"

"Anna, I've told you, I honest to God didn't see his face, it all happened so fast it was like a blur."

"Then how can you say this?"

"It's just a feeling I have, a strong one. His build, maybe his hair, his age. Something. A lot of things."

"So you're almost positive it was him but you're not positive," she repeated.

"Anna, don't talk to me like I'm nuts. I'm telling you the truth."

"And you think he followed us to the zoo?"

"If I'm right, he must have. He didn't just show up by accident."

"But why? What could he want?"

"I don't know."

"And he didn't tell you on the phone."

"No, like I told you it was just I had no right to interfere, he had the right to die, it was none of my business, I was using it for publicity."

"Oh my," she said, shaking her head. "He couldn't know you if he said that."

Alan turned on the motor.

"Don't hate me," she said. "Please don't hate me. I don't doubt you for a second, not a second, but he seemed...he seemed like such a nice person."

He started to come back at her with something in anger. But he didn't; he said nothing. Another thought was going through his head, one that was so obvious he was amazed it hadn't struck him before. That the guy he'd saved wanted only to die. And he, who'd killed an innocent girl, only wanted to live.

When he came back to his apartment that night, he half expected to find that the man had called again. He hadn't. And what Alan learned the next morning pushed the fellow out of his head.

Some days he didn't go to the *Breeze*'s Web site because he just didn't want the anxiety of knowing that something was in it about the crime. Other days he couldn't bear the anxiety of *not* knowing. The following morning, Monday, he started to walk past his computer to leave for work, but he stopped and logged on. And as the newspaper formed on the screen, one of the headlines on the front page read:

SUSHEELA KAPASI EVIDENCE BOX FOUND

The story, attributed largely to Mack McKinney, said that at the time the body was found the police in checking within a mile or so of the scene had found large tire marks on a sandy lane. They were thought to have been made by a truck or perhaps a motor home. The police had no reason to believe that something this far away had anything to do with the murder, and they had never made it public. Somehow the box in which the molds were kept had been misplaced. Recently McKinney had led a new search for it and had just found it in an old discarded locker.

Alan leaned back from the computer, trying to get his thinking straight. If they'd also found his footprints—maybe even one with bloodstains from his cut foot!—they would have mentioned it, wouldn't they? Or were they still keeping that a secret? As for the motor home, that surely was long gone, must have been crushed or taken apart in some junkyard. But could they somehow trace those tracks to a certain kind of motor home? And from there to the rental company—and then to him? It seemed so farfetched, but who knew?

He was about to turn off the computer when he decided to look at a few links he hadn't explored

before. And a four-word headline on the third one he
looked at grabbed at him.

POSSIBLE ANSWER AT LAST?

The story was about Harold Luder and the murders
he'd confessed to—and the ones he was being ques-
tioned about. And one of the victims they were trying
to link to him was Susheela Kapasi.

It kept changing, how he felt. Within the same few
minutes he could feel free, then that he'd been given
only a respite, for he knew that Luder could never ulti-
mately be tied in with the crime.

In the office that day he somehow did all the things
he had to do: look at mail, dictate letters, speak to
people, answer the phone.

One of the calls was from Anna.

"I just wanted you to know they asked me to stay on
for another shift. I didn't want you to call and find I'm
not home."

"Okay. I appreciate it."

She seemed to hesitate. Then, "Look, something
else. I want you to know he was here. He just left."

He started to say, "Who?"—the stranger was that
far from his mind. And then he said, a little startled,
"That guy?"

"Yes. He called and came over. He said he wanted
to see about the place for his aunt. He wanted to check
it out."

"And?"

"Well, his name's Bruster, Roy Bruster."

"Did he say where he lives?"

She thought. "No, I don't think so. No," definitely this time.

"Well, what did he say?"

"He said he liked it and that he's going to talk it over with her and I think with someone else." She paused. "Alan, please don't be mad at me. Please? But are you really sure it's him?"

"Look, I've told you, I've already told you what I think."

"I'm asking because it scares me."

"Why, did he say anything, do anything to scare you?"

"No, no, just the opposite. It's what you said about him that scares me. Like I said, he actually seems very nice. Our administrator even said it."

"Anna, I don't know what else to tell you."

"Look," she said, after some thought, "I really don't think he's dangerous. Unless, that is, he's crazy and I just don't see it. I don't see that at all. Can I ask you something? I almost don't want to…"

"Oh come on, just ask."

"If he kept calling you like that, I still don't understand why you haven't called the police? Or have you?"

"No. Like I told you. They wouldn't do anything. He didn't threaten me. And it's always from a payphone. They'd probably tell me to get an unlisted number. And that wouldn't do any good since he knows where I work."

She didn't say anything for a few moments. Then, "Look, I know if he's the same person he's an ingrate, and I'm angry at him for that, and there's got to be something wrong with him. But what I'm trying to say is that trying to commit suicide doesn't make someone a bad person. Just a tragic person."

Oh Anna, he thought. You've found another bird with a broken wing.

Chapter Thirty-Three

He was to chair a meeting of the division heads the next morning but, on impulse, the first thing he wanted to do when he got to the office was see if there was a telephone listing for a Roy Bruster in the city or suburbs. Or was it a phony name?

"I don't see any Roys," the operator told him, "but I do have an R Bruster. In Wayne." One of the suburbs. "Would you like that number?"

After jotting it down, he tried to think what to say when he made the call. He didn't want to talk to him, not yet anyway, just wanted to know where he could reach him if he ever wanted to. He decided he would simply ask whoever answered if R stood for Roy and, if it did, pretend to have the wrong Roy Bruster. He had to be prepared, however, that the guy himself might answer and recognize his voice. But all of this turned out to be a waste of anxiety; no one answered the phone.

He tried to think if there was anything else he could do, then looked over at his computer.

Whatever had driven that guy to try to kill himself, maybe a death in his family, a divorce, a crime—had he, too, committed a crime?—whatever it was, maybe there would be something about him in the newspaper.

Quickly he found the Web site for the city's largest daily paper. He had no idea if every crime, every obituary, if everything they published in the past few months, say, would be included in their online edition, but he typed in the name Roy Bruster and waited. It brought up nothing. He was thinking about trying the city's second largest daily when he heard:

"Alan?"

He looked up and Ron Jameson was standing in the doorway. He had a slight smile above his bowtie.

"Did you forget?"

Oh Christ. He was more than ten minutes late for the meeting.

He gathered up his briefcase and strode with Jameson down the hall and into the conference room. Elsa Tomlinson and the division heads were sitting on either side of the long conference table, Elsa next to the empty chair he was supposed to be in.

She was staring at him, hard. They were all staring at him.

He was scheduled to attend a three-day conference in Chicago the next morning. It was a conference of private school educators, and Elsa wanted him there primarily to mingle and learn. He took a plane that evening, anxious just to get away.

Wishing he could go even farther and longer.

Over the next three days he attended seminars,

gave a talk on the Foundation's goals, was almost always talking to people and yet found time to wander through the Field Museum. But anxiety was always hovering around, though it didn't really begin to close in until he was flying back through the night.

In all these years he had never shaken off the feeling that somewhere police would be waiting for him, this time on the tarmac or, again, at his apartment building. It was almost like something solid he always had to get through. Then when he was entering his apartment and saw the red light on his machine he was sure that one of the calls was from him—from Bruster.

But he had only one call, from Gregg, about "getting together."

The first thing he did was call Anna. And at the sound of her voice he sensed anger.

"Fine," she said when he asked how she was.

"Is there anything new?"

"No."

"Anna, is something wrong?"

She didn't answer right away. Then, "I didn't hear from you."

She was right: It hadn't been as if he had forgotten to call or was too busy. He'd just kept putting it off, consciously wanting to pull back a little from her. And yet that didn't make any sense at all; he was so anxious to talk to her now, to see her.

"Anna, all I can say is I'm sorry."

"I was worried about you. I thought something might have happened."

"Come on. Nothing happens to guys like me."

"Don't joke. I was looking forward to talking to you and you didn't call."

"Anna, I'm sorry."

"Did you," she asked hesitantly, "have a date?"

"Anna, please. No, I didn't have a date. I was always with people and—"

"Don't yell at me."

"Honey, I'm not yelling at you."

"You were. I don't want to be yelled at."

"I'm sorry if it sounded that way. I didn't mean it. Now, what are you doing? Can I see you?"

"You don't have to. I'm not a child."

"I know I don't have to. I want to. Can I see you?"

He got to her apartment a little before ten. She still seemed distant, and when he tried to kiss her she buried her face instead against his shoulder.

He said, "Anna, don't be mad at me. Please?"

"I'm not mad." But she didn't lift her face.

He wanted to say, "Then what's wrong?" But he knew what was really troubling her, that it was not all his not calling: She wanted him to say so much more than he could say.

She took a deep breath. "So tell me about Chicago," though he knew she was not interested in Chicago.

"It's a very beautiful city. With a beautiful lake that's more like an ocean. Have you ever been there?"

"No, I haven't been to most places."

"Well, tell me about your work. How's it going?"

She shrugged. "You know. What can I say?"

And then he asked her what he had told himself not to: "Did that guy Bruster's aunt ever show up?"

"No, in fact he called just today to say she was going to get live-in help for a while. He asked me if I knew anyone. I said I didn't." She paused. "I don't know if I should tell you this, it might upset you. But he asked me to go out with him. I told him no," she added quickly.

Alan looked at her, and as he did the strangest thought flashed through his brain.

That bastard's out to steal my life!

He came home shortly before one. Ordinarily he might have stayed over but when he held her and kissed her goodnight it seemed right—to her too, he sensed— that he go.

He hadn't checked the *Breeze* since leaving for Chicago and he didn't want to now either. He wanted to go right to bed, didn't think his head could absorb another thing. But when he was still awake a couple of hours later he couldn't resist the pull any longer and he went over to the computer. And there in the darkness of his living room glowed a picture of Mack McKinney holding flowers as he kneeled by a gravestone.

The headline read: FLOWERS FOR SUSHEELA.

The story told how yesterday would have been her twenty-eighth birthday, and that McKinney and occasionally other investigators visited her grave on that day. McKinney had started going following the death of her parents because she had no other relatives in this country. And he had never missed a birthday.

Alan kept staring at the picture, unable for long moments to turn it off.

Who in the end, he wondered, was going to drive him mad—the girl he murdered or the man he saved?

Chapter Thirty-Four

Both Patty and I couldn't get over Alan's behavior at the zoo, and we still occasionally brought it up. Like this one morning at breakfast, the morning I'd made a note to call Detective Murray again.

"I still keep thinking about it," Patty said. "I feel sorry for him that he's obviously jealous of her, but the thing that bothers me is that he didn't give two damns we were standing there able to hear. I felt so sorry for her. Has he ever talked to you about her?"

"No…"

"No you're relieved he hasn't? Or no you wish he would?"

"Pat, what the hell would I say to him? Give her up? Marry her?"

"I don't know. I guess just listen to what he may have to say."

After breakfast I went to my desk. I had a few things I wanted to check with Detective Murray but I learned that he was out and wouldn't be back until late in the day. He returned my call early in the evening. And before I even had a chance to ask him a question, he said, a weariness in his voice:

"The damn Luder thing is going all over the place.

Whatever you ask the prick did he do this, did he do that, he says yes. He doesn't want a lawyer and he's confessing to everything now, and we don't know where we're striking gold and where he's full of shit."

And this, I realized, could go on forever.

Gregg Osterly called Alan at the office late the next afternoon. "How about meeting me at the gym after work?"

"No, sorry." He had no desire to go. "I've got too many things to do."

"Come on, it'll do you good. And it'll do me good beating you at squash." Gregg finally talked him into it, and Alan wasn't sorry once he got there and into a game. It was as though that little ball became his enemy, the threat to his life, as he raced to it and smashed it from angles and off ricochets he had never made so consistently. He beat Gregg every game. Afterward, wiping his face with a towel, Gregg said, "Next time I ask you to come, stick to your guns. Don't come."

Alan started to go off to shower but he still had energy he hadn't used, so he walked past the noisy weight room, which was rimmed by a track, and swam lap after lap in the Olympic-size pool.

But the feeling of well-being lasted only until he started walking out of the building to his car. The car that was now taking him back to his life.

He wasn't in his apartment long when the phone rang. A woman's voice said, "Who is this?"

"Miss," he said, "you called me. Who are you?"

"Well, you called us a few days ago. I'm just curious and want to know why."

"Tell me, who is this?"

"Didn't you call a few days ago? The name's Bruster."

R. Bruster, of course! She must have had a phone system that identified all calls, even unanswered ones.

"Oh," he said, "yes, I did. And thanks for calling back."

"As I say, I'm just curious."

"Well, I'm trying to reach a Roy Bruster. And I was wondering if this is his number."

"Roy? No, this isn't Roy. You have the wrong person."

"Would you happen to know a Roy Bruster?"

She paused. "Look, I'm going to let you talk to my husband."

The line was silent for a few minutes. He didn't know whether she had quietly hung up or was conferring with someone. Her husband came on. He said, "Do you know Roy Bruster?"

"I met him briefly and I want to get in touch with him."

"What's your Roy look like?"

Alan gave him a fast description. After a long pause the man said, "Well, he and I are cousins. But we're not friends, you understand? In fact I haven't seen him in a long time."

"Do you know where he lives?"

"No."

"Well, can you tell me something about him? Do

you know, for instance, if he has an aunt he looks after?"

"An aunt? I don't know anything about an aunt. Maybe on his mother's side. I wouldn't know that."

"Do you know if he's married?"

"Look, I'll tell you this," he said, his voice suddenly angry—at Roy Bruster, Alan quickly learned. "The last I heard, he was married, had kids. But I'll tell you this too—he's crazy. He—" He stopped, and Alan could hear the vague sounds of an argument with his wife. He came back on, apparently warned by her. "Look, I've said enough. I don't need trouble. Good luck to you."

And with that he hung up.

Alan immediately called Anna. "Look, I don't want to be a pain but I thought you should know this." He then told her what he'd heard from Bruster's cousin. "He used the word crazy. I got the definite feeling he was afraid of him, even afraid just to talk about him."

She didn't answer right away. Then, "Well, I haven't heard from him again. And I don't think I will. But I'm going to say this again, I'm not afraid of him. In fact it's all just very sad."

"What do you mean sad?"

"Just that it's very sad." She hesitated. "When he was here he told me some things about himself but I didn't want to tell you, I knew how you felt. But a lot's happened to him. He lost his job as a teacher and after that he lost his wife and kids—she took off with them.

And to top it all he's come down with diabetes. He's a depressed guy and like I say it's sad."

He wanted to say just be careful of him but he didn't. He simply said something like, "I see."

There was a long pause, then she said, "Look, I hope you don't mind but I think I'm going to go to bed now. So look, you take care."

"You too, Anna."

And with that he sensed that this girl he loved and yet knew he had to push away had finally pushed back.

Chapter Thirty-Five

He felt emptied out, as though everything was gone now. There were only two people he could think of, my mother and me, who would be truly distressed by the magnitude of his secret—after all, we'd known him ever since he was a kid—and even we would get over it. His mother would never know; Anna, with him already out of her life, would come to realize something had been wrong with him all along; friends such as Gregg Osterly and people like Elsa Tomlinson would be shocked to their toes but it wouldn't change their lives one bit. He felt all of this, but nevertheless a phone call he got late the following afternoon almost lifted him from his chair in rage.

"Mr. Benning, this is Steve Manuso."

"Oh yes, Steve." The manager of the gym.

"Look, I just want you to know that a friend of yours was just here and went through the place to see if he might join. In fact he asked if he could use the pool as your guest and I told him he could. Anyway he says he's pretty sure he's going to join."

"Who's that?"

"A fellow named Bruster? I think it was that. Roy Bruster?"

"He was *there?*"

"Yes, that's what I'm telling you. Did I do wrong?"

"Steve, you should have called me, that's what you should have done. He used the *pool?*"

"Look, I tried calling you before I let him go through but I got no answer, and he seemed like such a nice guy I thought, why not. I'm sorry, that's all I can say, I'm sorry."

"Is he still there?"

"No, he isn't. God, I'm sorry. I can't begin to say."

"Look, he's not only no friend of mine, he's a liar, he's crazy. He comes there again using my name, you throw him out."

"Oh I goddamn will. Oh I will."

Alan's hand was shaking as he put down the phone. Frantically he was trying to think how that bastard could have known about the club, then realized he must have followed him there too. Oh, that bastard, that bastard! Crawling through his life! Taunting him! And now what next?

Meanwhile, something Patty had said to me stuck in my head.

Just listen to what he has to say.

No delving, no preaching, no moralizing, no advice, just listen to what he has to say. Hear him out, let him simply know you're there and always will be there for him.

I thought of him as a kid, how when he was five or six he liked coming over to my house and playing, say, Chinese checkers, or just watching TV with me, and then sleeping with me in my bed, even though we had other beds and though he claimed once that I snored. And my showing him how to ride a bike, and taking him to the movies, and once accompanying him and his friend Will Jansen into the nearby woods, which was really terrific of him to share with me. And playing ball on the driveway in back of our houses with other kids, most of them his age, a couple of them mine. And then when I got my driver's license, taking him out one July 4th to watch fireworks, and on the drive back letting him lean across me and steer.

It was all so long ago, but we still had something of that bond, didn't we?

So I called him one evening, and once again he answered the phone in a kind of angry way.

"It's just me, Alan, take it easy, it's just me."

"What did I do?" he demanded defensively. "What's that about taking it easy?"

"Just an expression. How are you?"

"Good, I'm fine." But he still sounded defensive.

I asked him about his work and he said he was enjoying it, and he asked about mine and I mentioned for the first time to him that I was looking into the life and crimes of Harold Luder.

The silence on his part that followed was so obvious.

I said, "Are you there?"

"Yes, I'm here." But it was halting. "I dropped something on the floor, had to pick it up."

And that sounded phony.

I wasn't sure what to say.

"Alan, is everything okay?"

Again silence. Then, "Of course everything's okay. Why?" He sounded a little angry,

I felt off balance. I knew I wasn't going to take this any further with him and I think we talked then about the news and a few other things that I forget.

It was a friendly goodbye. I remember saying, "Take it easy."

But he wasn't taking it easy when he hung up. Sitting at his desk he thought of me writing about Luder's crimes, and wondered anxiously what I might have found out. He berated himself for acting belligerent and nervous, and he wondered what I must be thinking. And almost in desperation he grabbed up the phone and called me back.

"Colin. Me. Look, I do have something on my mind. I'm sure you got a hint of it at the zoo. I don't know why I didn't tell you this before but I thought it would just disappear. But it hasn't. You remember that guy talking to Patty at the zoo?"

"Sure."

"Well, I think he's the same guy I saved in the subway. Where I was supposedly such a big hero. Anyway, he's been…well, I don't know if stalking's the right word, but it's good enough. He's been stalking me."

And he went on to tell me about the calls and the visit to the gym.

"And to top everything, here's Anna saying what a good guy he is and what a hard life he's had. And that got to me."

"Well, she's not only a nurse but she seems to be a very kind person, someone who sees good in everyone."

"Oh, I don't doubt that."

"Are you afraid he's cutting in?"

"God, if she lets him, he can have her."

"That's not what I asked. Are you afraid he's cutting in?"

"I guess it's part of the whole thing. That in a way he's out to take over my goddamn life. So why not that?"

"Let me ask you this. When he went to the nursing home, did he give them his name?"

"He gave a name—Bruster, Roy Bruster—but I don't know where he lives."

"Then why don't you call the police? I don't understand why you haven't."

"I was waiting to see if he bugs me again. But I will."

We both said nothing for a few moments. Then I said, "Hey, how about us getting together for dinner tomorrow? Just us. No serious talk at all. Unless you insist."

He laughed, which was good to hear. And then said okay.

But the laugh was gone almost the instant he hung up. He kept sitting at his desk. He'd wanted—oh, how he'd wanted—to say come over now, Colin, right now, and then to tell me everything—*everything*. For me to be the cousin he'd loved being with, sleeping with, facing my back with his little hand on my shoulder.

And to say, "Colin, I did it but I didn't mean it. Help me, help me."

Tonight, yes, tonight in his thinking. But would he do it tomorrow?

He stood up to do—what? He didn't want to watch TV. He couldn't bring himself to read a newspaper, let alone a magazine or book. Maybe jog—go outside and run and run.

Instead he logged onto the *Breeze*.

The main headline in today's paper read:

SUSHEELA KAPASI MURDER SOLVED?

And the story went on to say that Harold Luder had confessed to it.

He sat back as though shot. It was several moments before the thought sank in: *Free?* And to breathe God's air freely at last?

Chapter Thirty-Six

I met Alan for dinner the following day at an excellent Italian restaurant not far from his apartment. I got there about ten minutes before he did. He came straight from his office and looked it, in a dark blue suit, blue-striped shirt and Hermès tie. I smiled as we shook hands and I made a joke about me wearing a sweater, and he said he wished he could work like that.

He seemed to be in a great mood.

We ordered a half-carafe of chianti before looking at the menu, though I didn't realize until later that he didn't finish his first glass of wine.

Soon after we gave our orders and started talking we found we almost had to yell to be heard above the din in the small restaurant. Everyone seemed to be trying to shout above everyone else. We talked in spurts and with great effort, and after we finished the meal—he made me put away my credit card, insisted on paying—he said, "How about coming up to my place for a while? We can sit and relax a while and talk."

Outside he said, "This is the last time I go here. I've been here before and it was never that bad."

"Sorry, I can't hear yet."

He started to repeat, then laughed and we walked to our cars, to meet at his building.

What I didn't know was that he wanted to find out if I knew anything more about Harold Luder and his confession. But as it turned out he wouldn't have a chance to ask.

I met him in the parking lot and we took the elevator to his floor. And there, even before he put his key in the lock to his apartment, the door slid open a little with just his turning the knob.

He shot me a look, then stood there staring into the apartment through the small opening.

I said, quietly, "Could you have forgotten to lock it?"

"No, I'm positive I did."

"Did you double-lock it?"

"I think. I always do. Almost always do. But that I can't swear to."

I knew, of course, what he was thinking: If it wasn't double-locked, someone might have opened it with a plastic card.

He pushed the door all the way open with his foot. We both stood there apprehensively, staring into the living room; beyond that were a bedroom, a kitchen and bathroom.

Everything about the living room seemed untouched in the silence.

I was about to say, "Do you want to call the police?" when he went in hesitantly. I followed.

"Nothing," he said quietly, "looks touched."

We walked slowly through all the rooms. Everything still seemed untouched.

"You must have left it unlocked," I said.

He nodded. "Anyway I don't see how anyone could have even gotten into the building."

The apartment house was a four-story complex made up of four connected buildings, each with its own main entrance. You had to tap in your apartment's code number for the front door to unlock.

"Except," he said, "I've seen strangers walk in behind groups of tenants or people who are delivering something. All someone really has to do is wait and bluff."

With that he began opening drawers. But apparently nothing was missing.

We walked back to the living room from the bedroom, stood there looking around. And then all at once he strode over to an easy chair near one of his bookcases and picked up a book from the seat. He held it in his hand, a look of bewilderment on his face.

"This wasn't there when I left," he said, looking at me. "I know it."

"Maybe—"

"No maybes about it."

He began looking around the room again, almost wildly this time. Then I saw him staring at the computer on his desk, near one of the windows. It was turned off.

"I had that on!"

"Are you—"

"Don't ask me am I sure! I'm sure! I'm sure! I had a screen saver on. And the chair's pulled back. I didn't leave it like that!"

He strode to the computer, sat down and turned it on. The screen opened to the white desktop. He was sitting there staring at it for a long moment, as though trying to decide what to do, then spun as if aware for the first time that I was standing right behind him, looking at what he was doing. He began fumbling with the keyboard, finally turned off the machine.

"Sorry, I'm sorry," he said.

"What're you sorry about?"

"I don't know. I'm just so goddamn upset."

I looked at him as he kept staring at the dark screen. I said, "Look, did you call the cops on that guy, what's his name?"

He nodded, barely, almost as if he hadn't heard.

"Did you hear anything from them?"

"No." He still looked and sounded distracted.

"Are you going to call them about this?"

He nodded. But it was almost as if he was saying don't bother me.

"Look," I said, "what can I do?"

"Nothing. Nothing. You just go. I'll handle it."

Patty was reading a book in the living room when I got back to the apartment. She looked up with a smile. "Did you have a nice time?"

"Well, it started off nice."

I told her about the apparent break-in, and then about the guy at the zoo and the calls Alan had been getting.

"Oh that's so weird," she said, wincing. "And it's the same fellow Alan saved?"

"He's pretty sure it is."

"Oh that's crazy, that's maddening. He's called the police, hasn't he?"

"He says he did but he hasn't heard anything from them."

"How about on this? Did he call them?"

"Not while I was there. But he said he would."

"Why didn't he do it right away?"

"I don't know."

"Did you ask him why?"

"Pat, I don't know. I told you I don't know."

"Why are you annoyed at me?" she asked.

"Pat, I'm not annoyed at you. I'm sorry if it sounded that way. It's just upsetting. He's a big boy, though."

"The whole thing is crazy," she said.

I walked to my office and sat down at the desk. She came to the doorway and looked at me.

"Look, he's a big boy," I said again.

She stood there for a few more moments, then walked away. She was right, of course: It was crazy. Who the hell would break into his apartment and not steal anything, but leave clues—a book on an easy chair, a turned-off computer—clues to say he had been there? And I was also puzzled by something I hadn't thought to mention to Patty. That was the confusing scene at his computer, where he'd reacted almost in panic that I was looking over his shoulder.

All of that, and the calls he'd been getting, and him not just grabbing up the phone for the police...

I made up my mind not to give it any more thought. He wasn't, I told myself again, a kid anymore and I wasn't his big cousin protector. Still, I couldn't shake it from my mind even when I was in the shower. Particularly in the shower. With the water streaming over me, I began thinking again of him staring at his computer desktop and then trying to shut it down fast when he saw me looking over his shoulder. But I'd already seen that his desktop had just one icon on it in addition to the usual ones for the hard drive and trash: an icon for a site he obviously wanted to be able to get to quickly, that was important to him.

Why only one? And why the panic?

I had read what he'd labeled the icon, which I'd thought I had fixed in my brain at the time, but I was having trouble recalling it now. Part of it I was fairly sure of: breeze. But I just couldn't remember the first part.

I went to my computer and out of curiosity tried some possibilities. Goodbreeze—it had been something like that. Bestbreeze? Gladbreeze? After about fifteen minutes I quit and went to bed.

I fell asleep easily; I generally have no problem with that. But I woke in the dead of night. Patty was sleeping on her side, away from me. I lay on my back, staring into the blackness, wondering what had awakened me. I had no dreams that I remembered but I felt a kind of anxiety as if I'd had a nightmare. I kept staring up at the ceiling. And then the word just formed in my mind.

Codbreeze.

I closed my eyes, sure I would remember it, then opened them again, thinking of how many times I would completely forget dreams or ideas that I'd been sure I would recall in the morning. Careful not to disturb Patty I slipped out of bed.

In the glow of my desk lamp, I turned on the computer and typed "Codbreeze" into Google. Just one link appeared, something about breeding Hungarian dogs. That couldn't be it. At the top of the page, Google showed one of those helpful questions it asks when it thinks you've made a mistake—"Did you mean: _cod breeze_"—and I clicked on the underlined words. This time, a page of links appeared, mostly ads for Cape Cod vacation homes, but also, clustered right at the top of the page, a handful of links for a newspaper, the _Cape Cod Breeze_.

This was progress, in that it was conceivable that Alan might keep a link for a Cape Cod newspaper on his desktop. But why? Why not the _New York Times,_ say, or the _Washington Post,_ or some other large paper? I clicked through to the _Breeze_'s Web site and looked at the headline stories to see what the paper had to offer.

The articles offered no obvious clue to what Alan might have found interesting about the paper. They were the usual sort of news and features you'd find in any local paper. By now my head was becoming clouded again with sleep; I was even finding it hard to remember why I'd been so curious about this. But for the hell of it I tried clicking on a few more links to go deeper into the paper's archives. The pages loaded one by one. Regional News. Sports. Weather. Entertainment. Crime Blotter. And that's where I got my first glimpse of the story, though I didn't know what I was looking at yet. The headline said:

SUSHEELA KAPASI MURDER SOLVED?

At first I looked at it without any particular interest, but then I realized the name meant something to me. What was it? I remembered, then, that Susheela Kapasi was one of the girls Detective Murray said Harold Luder had confessed to killing.

Even then, though, I didn't make any connection with Alan. This, after all, was just one story out of many in the paper, and following murders was my beat, not his.

Chapter Thirty-Seven

Why, Alan kept lashing himself that night, had he acted so crazy in front of me? It was the zoo all over again, only worse. Like I had seen something, would suspect something, would do something.

His cousin Colin!

No, he tried assuring himself, I wasn't the one he had to be worried about. Had to be scared of. I wasn't the one who had broken in to his apartment, who had gone into his computer, maybe had even clicked on the goddamn icon that he should never have kept there in the first place; maybe had gone through the newspaper's site wondering, searching—seeing the stories, the sketch, and maybe having a sudden moment of comprehension. Even if Bruster—it had to be Bruster!—hadn't actually done that, he'd left a message as surely as if he had scrawled it on the wall:

I was here. I am in your life and I will learn your secrets.

His phone rang a little later, about ten-thirty, while he was sitting at his computer. He'd gone for a drink of water, he'd gone to the bathroom, he'd thought about getting in his car and just driving and driving. But he

had come back to his desk and so was still sitting there
when the phone rang.

He was afraid to reach for it, that it might be him,
and he let it ring until the machine picked up and he
heard Anna's voice. "Alan, it's me, I—"

He grabbed the phone. "I'm here."

"Alan, I miss you."

"Oh I miss you too." It just burst out of him.

"Can I come over?"

"No, no, I'll come there."

"I don't want to make you." She sounded as if she
had been crying.

"Don't be silly. I want to."

It wasn't fair, he told himself as he drove, this wasn't
fair to her at all, but he missed her, he loved her. And
when she opened her door for him, in a thin robe,
their arms came around each other and they kissed
hard. He closed the door with his foot.

In bed, he kept touching her hair, pushing it back
from her forehead as if he could never see enough of
her face. They kissed hard, then softly, then hard
again, breathing into each other, and now with their
tongues touching, rolling over one way and then the
other.

As he held onto her he forgot his anxiety and his
fear for the moment, felt only wave after wave of
blessed oblivion. Then as they sagged apart he kept
thinking *I must never lose this, must never lose her.
Never. Ever.*

Chapter Thirty-Eight

I didn't go back to bed, just fell asleep on the sofa. I woke early, about six, a little stiff and chilled; I hadn't used a blanket. After making sure the bedroom door was closed against any noise, I made coffee and brought it back with me to the office. I'd left the computer on, and within seconds I was looking again at SUSHEELA KAPASI MURDER SOLVED?

I began to read it; I hadn't made it past the second paragraph last night. When I finished I kept looking at the story—something made me keep coming back to it, something made me think this story was why the link was on Alan's desktop. I found myself thinking about the police finding tire tracks of what could have been a motor home, and about that weekend years ago I spent with my mother and her new husband at Sea Belle, when my uncle's motor home pulled up to the house.

Ordinarily I would never have connected the two. But I also remembered my uncle telling everyone they were going on to Cape Cod.

Patty came into my office in a robe. "What happened to you last night?"

"I don't know. I couldn't sleep and I tried doing some work and then finally fell asleep."

"That's not like you."

"I don't know. I guess my mind was too active."

It was only after she left for work that I began to feel guilty about not telling her what was in my head—the motor home, that they had gone to Cape Cod, Alan's interest in that newspaper.

It felt stupid, almost obscene, to think of Alan in connection with a murder. It had to be coincidence of some sort. My God, not only had he been a great kid but he grew up to be such a good person—soft-spoken, kind, with a nice quiet sense of humor. And look what he'd been tapped to do—run that Foundation. That said something about the man he'd become.

I remembered so clearly my aunt and uncle and Alan coming out of that motor home into the bright sun. I remembered their smiles, the greetings, the hugs, how Alan and I had slapped each other's hands lightly as we often did. I could picture him in shorts, barefoot, a handsome kid with those hollow cheeks I always wished I had, and black hair always neatly combed, and dark eyes and a nice smile. I remembered all of us on the beach, my feet in the hot sand, the feel of sand drifting through my fingers as I sat there. And then I thought, too, of my envy.

I can't emphasize enough how that motor home symbolized everything I felt about that family: The closeness, the sharing, the love for each other. As far as I was concerned, Alan had the greatest mother and father. His father not only was a distinguished lawyer, he *looked* it. His mother was like the emblem of all mothers whose sole devotion is to her family. Now don't mistake me, I loved my mother. I loved her loud laugh, loved that she was fun, that she would do anything for me. But I couldn't get over my feelings about all those boyfriends, and how I particularly despised her new husband, a gambler who looted her slim bank account—*our* bank account. So—and that motor home vacation only emphasized it—Alan and his family stood for everything solid and stable that my life with my mother did not.

Anyway—and why had I just about forgotten it?—hadn't Harold Luder already confessed to that poor girl's murder?

I tried to think about work. But I really had nothing to do, and my thoughts stayed on Alan—and soon in a different way. Thinking of him brought back some of the many stories I'd written about guys with wonderful backgrounds, with loving wives and great kids and jobs, who turned out to have committed the most heinous crimes.

Almost against my will, I logged into the newspaper's Web site again. I clicked through stories on the Crime Blotter page, scanning each article and feeling a sense of relief when they held nothing about the murder, nothing that could implicate my cousin. But then something else appeared on the screen, indeed seemed to burst upon it. Large.

The sketch.

Oh Alan!

°

Sam Haggerty called about an hour later. No hello, no good morning, which was his way of letting me know he was mad at me.

"I tried calling you. Didn't you get my message?"

"No, I'm sorry, I just came in." Though I had gotten it. And couldn't care less right now.

"Well anyway, I thought I'd hear from you about Nolan."

For a few moments I wondered who the hell Nolan was. Then I remembered that he was a guy who'd been sentenced to life a few days earlier for murdering his wife. But it was a crime without mystery, something that was essential to *Detective Eye* stories: Nolan had confessed immediately to the police.

"Sorry, but I didn't think it was anything for you," I said. It was almost impossible to think about this now.

"Yes, ordinarily. But I'm thinking about the wife's mother. From what I've been reading, she's been giving some good quotes."

I knew then, of course, what he wanted: A story under her byline about her daughter and grandchildren and the son-in-law she once loved. *Oh*, it would read somewhere, *if only I had trusted my instincts about him…*

I must have ghosted a couple of dozen of those kinds of stories for him: Wives of killers, sons of victims, neighbors of mass murderers…

"Well," I heard myself say, "I'll look into it and I'll let you know."

"You do that." And he was gone.

I sat for a while with my hands pressed against my forehead. I still couldn't fully believe it. After all, I tried telling myself, the sketch didn't really look that much like him, just a touch. But soon I thought of something that almost made me shudder at myself—because it had excited me for a few moments. And I'm ashamed to mention it even now.

That Alan…that Alan could be my book.

Chapter Thirty-Nine

From what I understand, Alan drove to the office that morning, thinking one thing: It wasn't just freedom he feared losing. It was Anna, he must never lose Anna!

But God, he might.

Bruster, somewhere out there, might not have learned anything about him from his computer while sitting there in the apartment. But even so, even so.

You're being paranoid, Alan tried telling himself. Still, he couldn't shake it out of his head. And even without this business about the computer, just the guy breaking in, just his taunting, his following him, even having the audacity to go to his gym—

The gym! Alan was startled by a thought he couldn't believe he hadn't had right away. He was about to grab up the phone when just then Elsa Tomlinson appeared in the doorway.

"Do you have a few minutes?"

But the few minutes turned into an hour, and after that there were other things to do. And then he didn't feel free enough until he was home to make whatever calls it would take.

The first was to his gym. A woman, the assistant manager, answered.

He said, "Is Steve there this evening?"

"I just came on, I don't know. Hold on."

The manager came on in a few minutes.

"Steve, I want to ask you something. When a person comes in as a guest, do you have them sign in?"

"Sure."

"Do you ask for an address?"

"We ask because we like to put them on our mailing list but they don't always do it and sometimes we forget to look."

"Could you tell me if that guy Roy Bruster gave his?"

"Sure. Hold on." Then when he came back: "Yes, I have it right here." And the manager gave him an address in one of the suburbs, Ardmore.

Alan set down the phone and looked at what he'd written. Yes, but now what? What was he going to do with it? And was it even a real address?

Alan called me after Patty and I had finished dinner and I had just helped clear away the dishes.

"Are you eating?"

"No. Just finished." It felt so weird talking to him as though nothing was wrong.

"Look"—and there was obvious nervousness in his voice—"I want you to know I called the cops."

"Good," I said, even though I felt he was lying. "What did they say?"

"You know. They'll look into it. But I don't have any faith in that."

"Well, who knows?" It was becoming harder talking to him.

"Look," he said, and the tremor in his voice was even more obvious, "I acted a little nuts with you. But I was very upset."

"I understand." Understand, hell. I didn't understand anything.

"I just wanted you to know that everything's okay now."

When I hung up, Patty was looking at me from the sink. I said, "That was Alan. He said he called the police but he doesn't think that'll go anywhere."

"Well, at least he called them."

I was upset and angry at myself that I didn't tell her I didn't believe a word of it. But here I was, again, protecting him.

I wished I could just talk to him about it, could say something like, "Alan, if it didn't happen tell me, I'll believe you. And if it did, tell me. It happened so long ago, and you were just a kid, and look at all you've accomplished since then, and they'll surely take that into consideration, and I'm behind you, and my mother's behind you, and everyone who knows and loves you will surely be behind you."

I began thinking of the times when he was, say, three or four, and I'd tell him things like, "Alan, I just came back from a trip to the moon." And he'd look at me with wonder and say, "Really, Colin?" Totally believed me. There'd been so many times like that. I wished I could say what I wanted to say now, and that even though he was grown, a man, he would believe me too.

I stood there, trying to think. And then on an impulse I went to the closet and took out a light jacket. As I was putting it on, Patty said, frowning, "Where you going?"

"I want to see Alan. He's still quite upset and I want to see what I can do."

I knew what her look was saying: Why not over the phone? But she said nothing.

I drove there, not knowing what I would say to him. I tried to think it out. He would wonder what the hell was I there for, and I guessed I would say you didn't sound right to me and I'm concerned about you. And maybe he would open up to me, just maybe. Or if he didn't, maybe I would come out with the coincidence of their going to the Cape that summer, and the sketch—the sketch. No, not maybe, I would! And maybe he would have a perfect explanation, and we'd even laugh about it. But what if my suspicions were right? Would he lie? Say you're crazy? Tell me to get the hell out of there? Maybe—who knew—even grab a knife?

For the first time I felt a little afraid of him.

Chapter Forty

After Alan phoned me he felt bad about having lied about calling the police. But he just didn't want me possibly wondering about his behavior.

He put on a windbreaker and started walking to the door. He told himself he only wanted to find out if he had Bruster's actual address, nothing more than that. Just to see for himself. But he paused as he was opening the door, stood there in thought for a few moments. Then he went to his bedroom and pulled open the night table drawer and took out the gun. Holding it in his hand, he looked down at the box of shells. He started to reach for it, then stopped. Then he picked up the box and put it in one of his windbreaker pockets. The gun went under his belt, partway in the back. Like he'd seen so many times in the movies.

Only he was never going to shoot anyone—God, he hadn't shot at anything since that blackbird.

But he wasn't going to let anyone kill him either.

I rang the buzzer for his apartment four or five times without getting an answer. I hadn't wanted to call him to say I'd like to come over, because I was afraid he might say no; had simply hoped he was still there after making that call to me.

I rang again, twice more. Still nothing.

I went back to my car, stood there looking up at the windows of his apartment. The living room blinds were slightly parted and I could see that a light was on. But the room looked somewhat faint in the darkness, perhaps because that light was the only one on.

I was angry at myself for forgetting to bring along my cell phone.

I told myself: Go up there and ring the bell again. Hold your finger on it for five minutes, even longer. But I knew I was just playing with the hope he was in. I was sure he was out of there. Gone. But I couldn't make myself leave.

I felt that it wasn't just nervousness I'd detected in his voice; it seemed, as I thought of it, more like desperation. I could almost feel that desperation through my skin. I tried to imagine what he might be thinking: that he'd done something terrible, but that ever since he'd lived a good life, that he had a girlfriend he cared about and a good job and a reputation, and that he would never voluntarily give all of this up. Never.

Alan had wondered if the address he'd been given even existed, but he found that it did. It was a two-story frame house on a block of widely separated houses. The place was dark except for a small light on the first floor in a back room. He sat in his parked car near a streetlight, aware that this still didn't mean Roy

Bruster lived there. He wanted to go up that path by the lawn and ring the bell, and if he answered just confront him. Or maybe not even say anything; just stare at him and leave. Or say, quietly—nothing that would bring the police—stay out of my life.

No, just stare at him.

He walked up the path to the door, which was on the side of the house and lit by an overhead light. The blinds over the door were closed. He rang the bell and waited, his heart going fast. But no one answered even after several rings.

Back on the sidewalk he looked at the house again, thinking he might catch someone peering out. But no.

He started to get back in the car, then looked at his watch. It was a little before nine. He was thinking of going up to a few other houses on the block to see if anyone knew Bruster, decided to try the houses on either side of this one to start. The woman who answered his ring at the first house simply looked through the drape and called through the closed window, "What do you want?"

"I'm looking for a Mr. Bruster and I was wondering—"

"No one in here." And the drape fell.

No one answered at the second house

He walked to the corner. The intersecting street was lined with stores, all of them closed except for a taproom at the far corner. There were only three people at the bar and no one at the tables. He stood at the end of the bar, waited until the bartender came over.

He said, "I wonder if you know a Roy Bruster. I lost

his address but I think he lives somewhere around here."

The man thought. "No, never heard of him." Then he said to the others, "Anyone here know a Roy Bruster?"

Two of them shook their heads. The third raised a finger as if asking permission to speak.

"It could be a guy I heard about," he said, "but I don't know."

A friend who lived down the block, he went on, had told him that one day last summer he and his son were playing chess on their patio when he noticed a man looking at them from the sidewalk.

"I never forgot this, it's that funny. This guy simply walks up and asks if they'd mind if he watched the game. My friend don't want him there, but what's he going to say? So, he says okay, and then this is funny"—the man turned to the others at the bar and grinned before looking back at Alan—"crazy but funny, but he just quietly takes over for the kid and beats my friend in like two moves. And my friend is quite a chess player."

Alan said, "Your friend didn't know him?"

"Not at all."

"So why do you think it might be Bruster?"

"Well, he introduced himself. Now it's been a long time but I'm sure my friend said something like Bruster. The reason I remember that," and he grinned and looked over at the bartender, "was that it sounded like brewery."

"Did he say anything about where he lives?"

"I don't think so, but the guy was walking, so it's probably somewhere around here."

Alan went back to his car and stared at the house again. Everything looked the same but he decided to try once more. He rang the bell, twice, and then noticed a stirring of the blinds. The door opened narrowly, just enough for him to see an elderly man's face behind the chain.

"What d'you want?"

"Is this the Brusters? Does a Roy Bruster live here?"

"No." Then, "Are you the one that rang before?"

"Yes, I—"

"I was in the tub," he said angrily. "This is no time to come ringing people's doors." He started to close the door.

"Wait, wait! He said he lived here, he—"

"Look, fellow, no one by that name lives here."

"Well, do you know anyone by that name?"

"No." And the door closed.

Alan stood for a few moments, just staring at the door. He was sure at first that the guy was lying. But then he was not so sure. Possibly Bruster, asked at the gym to give his address, had simply reached out for one close to his own. But where in this darkened neighborhood did he live?

He felt himself growing more desperate. He walked back to the sidewalk. He didn't want to leave, but soon the feeling grew that the man was staring at him from one of the windows, that he might even call the police.

Alan got in his car, started it reluctantly, and then began driving away slowly.

Soon, though, he was aware that he was driving fast, much faster than the speed limit. He immediately slowed down but his heart was still racing. He'd been fantasizing about confronting Bruster, and Bruster taunting him, and his anger and fear and frustration rising…

And then as he got out of his car in the driveway, he saw me walking back to my car.

I think we saw each other at the same time. He stood near his car as though frozen, staring at me. He looked a little disheveled; his hair, always so neatly combed, was mussed, and his windbreaker hung open.

I felt stupid, wasn't sure what to say. I only hoped my nervousness wouldn't show. He spoke first.

"What is it? Is something wrong?"

"I just want to talk to you."

"Why? What is it?"

"I didn't like the way you sounded on the phone, that's all."

"Why, how did I sound?"

"I don't know. Just something. But it worried me."

"There's nothing to worry about." He sounded angry. "There's nothing wrong."

"Well, I'm glad."

"Everything's fine," he insisted.

"Well, can I at least come in for a while?"

He looked at me for a long moment, as though

deciding what to say. Then he began walking to the door, and I accompanied him.

In his apartment he said, "I don't know what you thought you heard."

"Well, I'm glad it's nothing."

"I just called to tell you I called the police, that's all. I thought you'd want to know."

"Of course I did. What did they say?"

"I told you," he said, annoyed. "They'll let me know if anything."

I sat down on the sofa. He looked at me as if trying to decide if he should too. He sat down without taking off his windbreaker. It was as though he was telling me not to get too comfortable. I could feel myself growing more nervous.

I said, "How's Anna?"

"She's fine. Just fine."

I was running out of superficial things to ask. "And your work? How's it going?"

"Good. Everything's fine."

I don't know how I seemed to him, but my face felt hot and I wondered if it was red. I took a deep breath and said, "Alan, is there anything you want to tell me?"

He looked at me narrowly. "What do you mean?"

"Just that."

"That doesn't mean anything. What are you trying to say?"

I looked at him. "Alan, you're acting worried, I know you're worried. And I want to be on your side."

He kept staring at me. "I don't know what the hell

you're saying. What do you mean you want to be on my side? I've got no side. I don't know what you're talking about."

I was growing fully afraid of him but I'd gone too far to stop.

"Alan, I saw the sketch. Talk to me."

"Talk to you." That's all he said. But he said it as if I were crazy.

"I remember you and your mother and father stopping at our place on Sea Belle that summer. And your father mentioning you'd be going to Cape Cod."

He said nothing but now there was a frantic look in his eyes.

"You're crazy," he said. "I don't know what the hell you're talking about, but you're crazy."

I took another deep breath. Maybe more than one.

"You know," he said, "you're talking out of the top of your head."

"Really?" I kept staring at him. And then it burst out of me: "The girl, Alan. The girl!"

"What girl? What girl? You're crazy, you know?"

"Alan, I do know. Do you hear me, I *know!*"

"You're…"

He stopped and we both stood staring at each other. And then what happened next was so fast that I couldn't react to it. His right hand darted under his windbreaker and came up with a gun. Two hands held it pointed at my face. They were trembling.

His face over the gun was furious. I wanted to close

my eyes but couldn't. I thought: I'll grab it, I'll die fighting for it.

"Oh God."

The words came from him, like a soft cry. And now the gun came down, slowly. He kept looking at me for a few moments more, his face anguished. Then he turned and ran to the door.

It wasn't until he was in the car and was hurrying to start the motor that he became fully aware that he was still holding the gun. He put it on the seat next to him, horrified that he'd actually drawn it on me. It was only then that he realized that it wasn't loaded. But that didn't matter: He'd pulled it on me.

He put the gun on his lap. He knew what he had to do, and though his heart was beating hard he wasn't afraid.

He pulled away fast, not knowing where he was going, only that he had to find a place. He didn't want to do it on a public street, where people would gape at daybreak, or anywhere kids played or people shopped or drove by on their way to work. He thought of the woods and the creek where he and Will Jansen had played as kids; that seemed an ideal place to call it quits. But suddenly he couldn't clear his head enough to remember how to get there.

He drove on, still without knowing the way. Soon he had no idea what street he was on or what neighborhood he was in. He pulled to the curb to try to

clear his thinking. He leaned back against the head-
rest, exhausted. The image of him aiming the gun at
me was so loathsome, so ugly, that he could hardly
bear it. He tried to calm down, tried to concentrate on
his breathing. It was so heavy he had to breathe
through his mouth. He was only partly aware that he
was looking at the sky. The moon, a half moon, was
out, which came as a surprise: He could have been
wrong but he felt as if he'd been driving through a
moonless night.

He looked at it, thinking: No more. Never again.

He closed his eyes but couldn't keep them closed.
What was starting to come into his head now terrified
him. It was a terror far different from anything he'd
felt before. And yet it seemed right to him. He felt his
head clearing, began to have some idea of where he
was. He started driving again, through streets he rec-
ognized now. And drove deep into the night.

For a long while he tried not to let a clear thought
into his head. And then when thoughts started to break
through they were jumbled. They were about Anna
and him and how much he loved her. They were about
his mother and his relief that she'd never know, at least
on this earth. They were about his father and did he
somehow know and could he help him, perhaps with
God. They were a little bit about Bruster too, but with
a touch of pity this time for all that he was suffering.

And hovering over everything, as if she were a solid
presence in the car, were so many thoughts of
Susheela.

Dawn was breaking, and he stopped once for gas and then stopped again, later, to ask something of two people he saw walking. And not long afterward he was parked in front of a house he'd been directed to. He stared at it from the car, scared again—the fear had receded for a long while as he drove. Fighting for calm, he got out and walked up the few steps and rang the bell.

He had to ring twice before someone came to the door.

He said, "Mr. McKinney?"

"Yes."

He said, "Mr. McKinney? My name is Alan Benning. I'm Alan Benning, and you've been looking for me."

Chapter Forty-One

McKinney looked puzzled.

"I don't understand. Who are you? What do you want?"

"Let me talk to you. I killed someone. I killed Susheela Kapasi."

Only a slight lifting of his heavy eyebrows revealed anything of what McKinney felt. He stepped back, and after Alan walked in and he'd closed the door, he gestured him to a chair, as if Alan were any guest in his home. Alan was still nearly frozen with fear but he felt it easing a little. The man looked almost gentle, dressed in rumpled trousers, a sweater and slippers. The living room had things of the sea on the walls, a fisherman's net, a large glossy fish, a painting of two geese flying over water.

On one of the lamp tables was a portrait of his daughter.

McKinney asked him his name again, where he lived, what was his work, did he have a lawyer.

"No, and I don't want one. I just want to plead guilty."

"You still have to have a lawyer."

"Then I'll get one."

"By the way, are you hungry, thirsty?"

"I could use a drink of water. Thank you."

McKinney left, and soon afterward his wife came into the room, in a bathrobe, and nodded at Alan. It was a few minutes before he was back, with a glass of water. After Alan finished it, he noticed that she was gone.

"So tell me more about yourself," McKinney was saying. "Are you married?"

"No, I'm not."

It continued like this, as if it were any conversation between friends, until the doorbell rang. McKinney stood up and went over to open the door. And the whole room seemed to change as South Minton's captain of detectives and two uniformed officers strode in.

A minute later Alan's hands were behind his back in handcuffs. And now hard fingers were gripping his forearm, leading him down the front steps and over to a police car.

And already alerted and waiting outside the police station was the first of what was to be an endless horde of TV cameramen and reporters. A reporter, a young man, walked along near him, calling, "Did you kill her? Did you kill her?"

The captain, a husky man with a buzz haircut, seemed a little startled. He had read Alan his Miranda rights and Alan had answered, "It doesn't matter, I don't want a lawyer, I just want to tell it."

The officer said, "I don't have to say this, but are you sure?"

He nodded. They were in a small room in the police

station, Alan and the captain seated at a table, a uniformed officer standing by the wall. Alan's heart was racing. Gone was the near calm he had begun to feel at McKinney's. In fact he'd half expected him to be here too, though he knew McKinney wasn't on the police force.

The captain, whose name was Johnson, said, "We'd like to tape record this, okay?"

"All right." His voice sounded hollow to him, as if his ears were stuffed.

"All right, now tell me."

All at once Alan was confused about where to begin. He put his fingers in his hair as if he could feel coherent thoughts. "I was on this path at the beach and I saw her and she'd lost her kite…"

The captain looked at him as his voice trailed off. He said, "Why don't you tell me what you were doing there in the first place?"

Alan had to go back in his mind, and finally he began to tell him about his mother and father and the motor home, and then his going to the beach with them and then jogging by himself in the woods. And after he told him that he'd touched her on the outside of her bathing suit, the captain said, "You're not telling me everything. You touched her underneath her suit too, didn't you?"

Alan rubbed his forehead, surprised he knew, and then nodded. It was as though touching her there was the thing he was most ashamed to talk about.

"Are you saying you did?"

"Yes."

After Alan told him everything he could remember, the captain said, "Why didn't you give yourself up long before this?"

"I really kidded myself into thinking maybe I hadn't killed her." Alan was looking at him earnestly.

"How could you think that? Her neck was almost broken."

"I don't know, I don't know."

"Did you want to rape her?"

"No! No! I don't know what happened, I just wanted to touch her."

"You didn't stop because you heard her father calling her?"

"No. I never heard him."

"Come on, the truth." It was the first time the officer's voice became stern.

"It is the truth. I swear."

"And you killed her so she couldn't talk?"

"I just couldn't stand everyone knowing."

"You could have just run away. You say you were parked a half-mile away. Your parents wouldn't have known."

"I know. I didn't think. I keep telling myself that over and over again."

"Why did you give yourself up now?"

"It was either that or kill myself. I didn't want to die."

The officer looked at him quizzically. Alan could almost read his thinking: But you were able to kill *her*, weren't you? Instead he said, "Let me ask you this. Why did you go to McKinney?"

For a few moments he couldn't think why this would matter. Then he remembered the newspaper story denying there was any friction between the two men.

He said, "I don't know." But actually he didn't want to tell the truth. It would have sounded phony, and anyway he wasn't sure how to say it. That it had something to do with the old officer having lost his daughter, that it was as though he owed him something.

In any event, Alan was never to talk with McKinney again.

In a cell for the first time, he had to struggle against the feeling that not enough air was coming through the bars. He sat on the edge of the hard cot, trying to calm himself and to concentrate only on breathing. It was the police station lockup, and no one was in the two other cells. In the silence he was thinking of how news of his arrest must be spreading; he even began picturing a mob gathered on the sidewalk outside. But never for a second did he regret confessing or not waiting until he had a lawyer.

I was the first person from his old life to see him. He looked at me dazedly when he was brought into the room where they let me meet him. He turned his head away quickly, and I said, "Alan, don't," and he looked back, tears in his eyes. I couldn't help it, but though I was still in shock and dismay at what he'd done, I began to cry too, not much but enough that I had to bring my wrist to my eyes to wipe away tears.

The first thing he said to me was he was sorry about pulling a gun on me.

"Don't even think about it," I said. "I don't."

"I'm sorry, I'm so sorry."

"I said don't think about it. I mean it. I understand. I came on so strong."

"Tell me how my mother is."

"She's okay. My mother went to see her. She's the same."

"She can't know, can she?"

"No, not at all. Don't worry about that. Look, I hear you don't have a lawyer."

"No, and I don't want one."

"Alan, you've got to have one."

"I really don't want one."

He never asked me about anyone other than his mother, or if I'd talked with Anna, which I hadn't, or if I had been in touch with anyone else he knew. It was as if that life was already over for him. I'd been told we couldn't touch each other, so I don't know if he would have let me embrace him. I know he didn't try to embrace me.

Walking out of the room, my legs were shaky. I would have gladly leaned against a wall in the corridor, but I didn't, just kept going till I was outside.

He never changed his mind about not wanting a lawyer, but I spoke with a member of his old law firm and he got one on the Cape to represent him. She was young, bright and tough—especially with Alan, when he told her he just wanted to plead guilty, didn't even want her to try for bail. But since that meant life without parole for first-degree murder, she hoped to convince him to go to trial.

Much was made in the news about his being a vice president of the Foundation, that he had saved a life, that he'd given himself up. I was interviewed several times by reporters, and I spoke of his character, of growing up with him, everything I knew of the person within him. There were also interviews with Elsa Tomlinson, who spoke kindly of him, and with Gregg Osterly and a few other friends, who had only good things to say. The reporters heard of Anna, but they couldn't reach her: She had left her job, and her family claimed not to know where she was.

Roy Bruster, too, had disappeared: He moved out of the house he'd been renting and I was never able to find him. From what I heard, he did indeed have a hard life. His father took off before Bruster was born, and his mother died when he was about four. He lived in a series of foster homes, and went for a long while to a school for disturbed children. He managed to go to college and get married, but though he taught high school math for several years, he was let go for some unrevealed reason and then held a scattering of jobs, mostly as a salesman. Then, just a year before his suicide attempt, his wife took off with their two children. And then there was the diabetes.

Alan received a stream of letters of support, of

prayers for him, and a few that came close to marriage proposals. But there were many more of another type.

There was story after story about Susheela, about the brilliant student and kind and lovely young person she'd been. Her murder was blamed for the deaths of her parents: Her mother's heart attack, of course, and it was even suggested that her father's automobile accident might have been suicide. And something came out that the police had never revealed before, that when they'd examined the body they'd found a fresh, long scratch on her groin, which seemed to confirm that Alan had intended to rape her before either being interrupted or, if you were disposed to be charitable to him, changing his mind.

And there were other things. One was his "temper"—the fight he'd had with the fellow in the parking lot, how he was "forever" threatening his next-door neighbor for playing music above a "whisper." A few of his neighbors and colleagues, sudden stars on TV, even spoke of things he'd never thought about himself, such as his being "aloof," "argumentative." Why, even his working for the Foundation came under some attack, like he'd stained it, like he was a hypocrite, had used it to try to cleanse himself. And then there was the interview with his old friend from childhood, Will Jansen.

Alan remembered him as a fairly tall, skinny kid like himself, but now in his early thirties he turned out to be only five-seven and heavy and almost completely bald.

Will told of so many good things, about them going

to the woods and the creek together, building model airplanes, doing homework together, never having a quarrel. But he also told of them "kidnapping" that little boy and sending him for "pigeon milk."

"He talked me into doing it," Will said, "and I did. But I never felt the same about him after that."

Chapter Forty-Two

Many if not most of you know something of what happened afterward. But certainly not all of it—far from all of it. One of the things you may know is that, since Alan was fifteen at the time of the crime, his lawyer tried but failed to have the case handled in juvenile court. At his trial he was found guilty of second-degree murder, which carried a life sentence but he would be eligible for parole after fifteen years.

Anna came to see him in prison as soon as she was allowed to after he was sentenced. They looked at each other through the glass that separated them, phones to their ears but not speaking right away. She was wearing, as he was to tell me, a light blue raincoat, and her blond hair had a faint glisten of rain to it. Her face, always pale, was never more so. Her eyes immediately filled up, and his started to also.

"How are you doing?" she managed to say.

"Okay. Just fine. I'm doing fine."

"Are you, are you telling me the truth?"

He was sure she was referring to the hard time that sex offenders, particularly the murderers of children, go through in prison. "Yes, I'm telling the truth."

"Do they let you see any counselors?"

"Not yet, but I think they may."

"Do you go to church services?"

"No." But he would soon, off and on. He then said, "Anna, this is a long trip for you."

"I don't mind. Alan, I love you."

"Oh Anna." He felt himself tearing up again. He wanted to cry out I love you too. But, he thought, how can I? How dare I?

"You try to take care of yourself," she said. "Do you hear me?"

"I hear you. I will."

She stood up, held up her palm and smiled. And then left.

He wrote to her soon after the visit, telling her in the most painful letter he'd ever written to go on with her life, that he had too many years here ahead of him. Perhaps the letter did it. Perhaps it was pressure from her family. Perhaps she found someone else. Perhaps all of it. Anyway, he never saw or heard from her again.

I know all this because years later, after a lot of red tape was cut, I was able to meet with Alan enough times for him to tell this story. It was his idea, and once he started it just about poured out of him, as if he'd held it in too long. To be honest I must admit that I often wondered, listening to him, how much of what he was saying was self-serving, until one day he said, leaning forward, his hands clenched on his knees, that no one but himself was to blame for him committing murder.

"A lot of guys have parents who're uptight about

sex," he said to me, "who never talk to them about it, but they don't go on to do what I did."

"Well, it certainly didn't help," I said.

"Perhaps," he answered slowly, "but I still have no one to blame but myself. No one."

It was shortly after this, in the thirteenth year of his sentence, that I got a call from someone in the prison, since his mother had died and I was listed as next of kin, that Alan was dead. His throat had been cut by another prisoner.

The belief is that Alan was another victim of his own crime, that he was killed because he was a murderous pedophile. The man who killed him, though, said that Alan was the one who had provoked the fight, that he'd started punching him for no reason, even though he knew the guy had a shiv. No one else witnessed it, so who really knows? But my own belief, based in part on the fact that he was killed soon after he finished telling me all he wanted to of his life, is that he wanted to die even though he would be eligible for parole in a couple of years. Or maybe *because* this was coming up. Perhaps Alan, with gray in his hair now but with the same gentle and troubled way about him, didn't want to go out into a world where the tag murderer and pedophile would be attached to him wherever he moved. But more likely, and this I do believe, he felt he hadn't been punished enough.

I think often of what he told me about his parents being blameless. I am not, however, that easy on myself. I think of all the times when he was a kid that I could have pointed the way, perhaps helped him bear his burdens, explained something or other. In other words, really been there for him. *Really* been there. The big cousin. The big brother. But they're long gone, those chances.

What I've often told my wife—one of our two children, incidentally, is named Alan—is that he is, in a sense, responsible for everything I write and will write. Everything. Even if *Detective Eye* were still around, and on the impossible chance I was still contributing to it, he would even be present as I wrote those stories, too.

As for Anna, let me say this:

"I think of her so often," Alan told me. "So often." And once: "I often wonder where she is, if she has a family, if she's content. Oh, I hope so. I owe her so much—that through her I came to know the joy and richness of life."

His regret was that he never really told her. My hope is that she will find out now.

THE
END

More Great Books From
HARD CASE CRIME!

Grifter's Game
by LAWRENCE BLOCK
MWA GRANDMASTER

Con man Joe Marlin accidentally steals a suitcase full of heroin, then plots to kill the man he stole it from—with help from the man's wife!

Top of the Heap
by ERLE STANLEY GARDNER
CREATOR OF PERRY MASON

The client had a perfect alibi for the night Maureen Auburn disappeared—but nothing made P.I. Donald Lam suspicious like a perfect alibi.

Two for the Money
by MAX ALLAN COLLINS
AUTHOR OF 'ROAD TO PERDITION'

After 16 years on the run, will Nolan bury the hatchet with the Mob—or will they bury him first?

To order, visit www.HardCaseCrime.com or call 1-800-481-9191 (10am to 9pm EST).
Each title just $6.99 ($8.99 in Canada), plus shipping and handling.